Allegra

Jenny Worstall

For music lovers everywhere

Contents

Chapter 1

An Unexpected Meeting
September

She saw him before he saw her. The width of his shoulders, the dark shiny curls creeping over his collar, that particular way of standing – all unmistakeable.

He turned round. "Allegra?" And frowned. "It is you! Allegra – long time no see."

"Aren't you going to introduce me?" Allegra looked at the tall blonde beside Zack.

"Of course! Allegra, this is Vanessa; Vanessa, meet Allegra."

Vanessa smiled, displaying perfectly even teeth. "Charmed! Come on Zack; we need to get going. Our flight's already been called. Switzerland awaits us!"

"OK honey." Zack picked up his battered leather case; he always took his precious musical scores as hand luggage.

Allegra dug her nails into her hand.

With such an early start, she hadn't made any sort of effort with her appearance. She must look a complete frump. As if Zack would have any interest in how she looked.

It had been a whole twelve months – an entire year – since she had last seen Zack and she had to bump into him at Gatwick at seven in the morning, with an extremely pretty girl on his arm. It wasn't the way she had imagined, meeting up again with the love of her life. Not at all.

"Orange juice? Certainly madam. With ice?"

Allegra accepted the drink gratefully and turned to face her friend Holly as they sat together in the plane.

"Here's to us," Holly said as she touched her plastic cup against Allegra's. "Doesn't quite sound the same as glass, does it?"

Allegra grinned. "Here's to a great trip to Barcelona. I hear the concert hall's beautiful."

"Certainly is," Holly replied. "Air-conditioned too, from what I remember. I played there last year, with another orchestra. Hotel was comfortable as well."

Allegra settled back in her seat, adjusting it so that she was reclining.

"Did you find what you wanted in duty free?" she asked Holly.

"I had a ball! Made a good start on my Christmas list. Surprised you didn't join me."

"I wanted to get on with reading my Kindle." Allegra shuffled a little in her seat. "You'll never guess who I chanced upon, when I was looking for a place to sit down in the waiting area next to the shops."

"Brad Pitt?"

Allegra shook her head.

"The Tooth Fairy? No? What about Genghis Khan? It's no good, you'll have to tell me, Allegra. I'm not a mind reader."

Allegra bit her lip and stared out of the window at a bunch of fluffy clouds in the shape of a large sofa. What she wouldn't give to be floating out there, all thoughts of Zack banished from her mind – forever.

"What is it?" Holly put her hand on Allegra's arm. "Who did you see?"

"You have to guess," Allegra replied. "A well-known musician. A conductor."

"Not that awesome young woman who conducted the first night of the Proms this year?" Holly's eyes sparkled. "She's amazing – I would have asked for her autograph."

"No. A man."

"Not...oh, Allegra, was it...?"

"Yes." The tears threatened to flow then.

Not now, Allegra thought fiercely. I'm not going to let myself cry in public.

Holly's hand moved again to pat Allegra. "Please don't be upset," she said. "It's not worth it. Whatever happened between you is over. You have to forget him – you deserve better."

"I don't care anymore. It was just the shock of seeing him, that's all."

Allegra turned her head to the side. "Think I'll

have a little snooze. It's a busy time ahead of us, with rehearsals and two concerts to pack into the next few days, so I need to re-charge my batteries."

It was easy to lie, to say she didn't care any-more, but it wasn't true and Allegra knew it. Her thoughts on waking every morning were for Zack. He occupied her mind and heart every moment of every day, and he was her last thought before sleep. She'd tried to forget him, but without success. She'd even been on a few dates with other men, mostly engineered by Holly in an attempt to help her move on, but they'd all come to nothing. She'd met some perfectly pleasant men but they all had one fault in common, a fault she found it im-possible to overlook – they weren't Zack.

But Zack seemed to be coping fine. Vanesa's perfect face appeared in front of Allegra and she opened her eyes quickly, to make it disappear.

Vanessa was about as different from Allegra as it was possible to be. She had the sort of looks models aspire to, and her hair – how on earth did she get it to be so straight and shiny, especially at that hour of the morning?

"Holly?" Allegra sat up and stretched her legs out – as much as was possible in the budget seats.

"I'm here." Holly put down her magazine. "Ready and waiting. I knew you'd want to talk."

Allegra smiled. "You're such a good friend. I promise I won't go on and on about this..."

"You can go on about it as much as you want."

"No, I mustn't. It's not fair on you and I need to

put him out of my mind, I know that. It'll probably be easier for me to forget him now."

Holly drummed her nails on the little plastic table in front of her.

"Easier? You mean because you've seen him again? I thought the opposite would be true – I thought seeing him again might stir up old memories."

"No, it'll be easier now," Allegra insisted, "because I saw it, on her finger, the ring – Zack's grandmother's ruby ring, the engagement ring."

"The ring?" Holly gasped. "You mean the ring you..."

"...yes, the ring I threw back in his face a year ago, when we split up."

Chapter 2

Time To Worry?

"Have you heard from Allegra? Has the plane landed yet?"

Cathy, Allegra's mother, was sitting with her husband Pete in the kitchen of their home in Bath.

"Relax," Pete said. "She'll contact us when she can. And she is twenty five, you know! She doesn't have to account for her every move. Allegra's grown up, with a proper job, in case you'd forgotten. And she's travelling with Holly, no doubt with lots of other colleagues too, so what could go wrong?"

Cathy sighed. "I know you think I worry too much and it's not as if I think anything's going to go *wrong* exactly, but I like to know when she arrives after a journey, especially when it's abroad, and especially when she flies."

Pete put his hand out to Cathy and she clutched it gratefully. "Most of what you worry about will never happen."

"But look what *did* happen..." Cathy began. "I don't think she's ever totally recovered from all that business with Zack." She fiddled with one of her earrings distractedly. "He seemed such a suitable partner for her, with their shared interest in music and so on. They were going to build a life together."

"He wasn't right for her," Pete said. "Not good enough for our Allegra, truth be told. I never thought it would work."

"Yes you did." Cathy smiled. "Your memory's playing tricks now, Pete. You said you were proud he was going to be your son-in-law. Kept going on about him, saying how pleased you were, your daughter going to marry an up-and-coming orchestral conductor. Not to mention the countless jokes you used to make when he was here about collecting fares, as if he were a bus conductor! You were looking forward to having Zack as your son-in-law. The son you never had."

"Not how I remember it, not at all." Pete coughed and repeated obstinately, "Not good enough for her. But at least she's over him."

"Is she?" Cathy asked. "I've never thought so. She seems different, more subdued somehow. Lost her sparkle."

"Maybe. But it doesn't do to dwell on it."

"My dearest wish is that she should meet someone else, someone who'll sweep her off her feet."

"It'll happen. Give it time," Pete said.

"But it's been a year already. Time's ticking on, the biological clock..."

"Now you're being silly," Pete said and put his arms round his wife. "Allegra's got a very bright future ahead of her; it'll all work out in the end, you'll see. She's bound to meet plenty of new people in that job of hers, rattling round the world as she does. One of them will be right for her."

"It was easy for us," Cathy said, "meeting in our first week at college, then both going on to be teachers in nearby schools."

"We were lucky," Pete agreed.

Cathy looked at the photograph of their wedding day sitting proudly on the dresser. Two faces smiled at her, both a little slimmer and quite a lot younger, but with the same expression of love beaming out of them.

Next to the wedding photo was a picture of Allegra taken when she was ten, a serious expression on her face, playing a solo on her violin, wearing a long frilly blue dress and white shoes. Her talent and dedication had meant a busy and exciting time for the family as they took her hither and thither for lessons, rehearsal and concerts, and when Allegra had graduated top of her class from the Royal College of Music, Cathy and Pete had been overwhelmed with joy and pride.

A sudden beep came from Cathy's phone.

"I bet that's her now," Pete said.

Hi Mum and Dad! I've arrived safely with Holly, after an uneventful journey. It's so much hotter here than the UK – glad I brought lighter clothes. Our hotel room is lovely and nearly as big as our whole flat in London!

Got to dash – rehearsal shortly. Another rehearsal

and concert tomorrow.

A x

PS Holly sends her best wishes.

"What did I tell you?" Pete said, reading over Cathy's shoulder. "Now, I'd better be off – need to be at the golf club in half an hour."

"Can't think why you're bothering," Cathy said. "You said you hated golf, couldn't understand why grown men would chase a tiny ball around a vast stretch of grass with a metal stick all day for no good reason."

Pete raised an eyebrow. "I said that?"

"Yes – you did!"

"Nevertheless, thought I'd give it a go. I've been offered another guest pass for the day so I might as well use it."

"Have a good time," Cathy called to Pete as he left. "Hope it doesn't rain."

She reckoned Pete must be finding his retirement more tedious than he was letting on if he was prepared to try golf again.

A quick glance at her watch told Cathy she too should be moving. She'd also recently retired, but whereas Pete was casting around somewhat forlornly for activities to occupy his time, her timetable seemed to have filled up all on its own, straight to bursting point.

Cathy picked up her bag and took her coatigan from the back of the chair. She was all set to go.

Hang on, nearly forgot my phone, she thought. That would have been a disaster.

She soon arrived at St Mildred's Charity Shop, where she was due to cover a shift for a sick friend.

"Hello! Tea?" Maeve, one of Cathy's closest friends, rushed towards her, arms full of a jumble of garments with three pairs of shoes balanced precariously on the top.

"Have we got time?" Cathy asked. "There seems so much to do."

"Of course we've got time." Maeve roared with laughter. "Life isn't worth living if you haven't time for tea. Now, be a dear and stick the kettle on."

Cathy did as she was told and soon the two friends were happily sorting and chatting, while sipping their favourite Earl Grey.

"Look at this," Maeve said, holding a tattered purple-sequined net micro-skirt across her ample hips. "Think it suits me?"

"How can I put this tactfully," Cathy began. "I can't, so no! It doesn't suit you – anymore than *this* suits me."

She flung a full-length bright pink fake-fur across her shoulder and rolled her eyes suggestively.

Maeve hooted and plonked an Austrian style hat with a feather onto Cathy's head.

"Maybe with this? Or this, perhaps," she suggested, adding a shredded silk scarf in vibrant colours.

"Hang on," Cathy wheezed. "You've got to stop making me laugh."

"Why?" Maeve demanded.

"Because my phone beeped," Cathy said. "I must have a text. Better check it in case anything's wrong."

She picked up her phone.

"Wait a minute," she said. "This is Pete's phone. Mine's in my bag as well. He must have left his on the table and I brought them both out by mistake."

"Never mind." Maeve started tidying up the mess they'd created. "The man can do without his phone for a day, can't he?"

"I'm sure he can, but that's not what concerns me." Cathy squinted at the small screen, not quite able to believe her eyes.

Maeve priced the Austrian hat at £2.50 and arranged it on a nearby shelf. "And what, pray, *is* concerning you?"

Cathy held Pete's phone up to show to Maeve. "Who's Alice," she asked, "and why is she saying to my husband 'See you soon'?"

Chapter 3

Rehearsal In Barcelona

The sound of excited chatter and instruments of all shapes and sizes being put through their paces was deafening as Allegra pushed open the door with her back, carefully cradling her violin and bow.

"Not too late!" Holly gave a sigh of relief. "Thought the taxi driver would never get us here in time."

After a delayed landing, the two friends had made their way from Barcelona airport to their hotel, dumped their bags, and rushed to the concert hall in the city centre for the first rehearsal. They slipped across the stage to the back of the first violins and sat down hastily.

"Look! There's the flautist I met in Rome last week." Allegra waved cheerfully to a petite woman in a purple dress.

"And over there – isn't he the double bass player from Dubai?" Holly grinned. "Was hoping I'd see him again."

"Quiet, ladies and gentlemen, please." The orchestra manager looked round at the musicians until he had their full attention, before continuing in the deepest bass voice, with a teensy hint of a soft welsh lilt, "May I welcome Maestro Rostopovsky?"

The orchestra gave a cheer as a diminutive figure clad entirely in black shuffled onto the podium.

"Good afternoon," he began, taking a small bow and clutching his hand to his heart. "I'm delighted to be here and cannot wait for our concert tomorrow. My beloved Beethoven – what could be better?"

Maestro Rostopovsky coughed, then raised his baton in a gnarled claw-like hand. "Let's play!"

The orchestra leapt into action and the familiar opening of Beethoven's Fifth Symphony filled the auditorium. "Da da da dah..."

Allegra relaxed into the piece. She would never tire of listening to Beethoven – each time she was asked to play this gem it seemed as fresh to her ears as the first time she'd heard it, aged seven, listening to a concert on the radio with her father. She had sat quite still, in a trance, as she'd listened. Pete had been amazed at her reaction and had started taking her regularly to classical concerts in Bristol after that.

Maestro Rostopovsky wiped his face with a large handkerchief during a pause in the music.

"He looks a bit tired," Holly whispered to Allegra.

"He's pulling at his collar," she replied. "He doesn't look terribly comfortable, does he?"

"It is rather airless in here," Holly said. "So much

hotter than England. Oh, here we go. Starting again..."

During the mid-rehearsal break, Holly and Allegra took the chance to nip outside and get some fresh air. Quite a few of the players were already outside, drinking glasses of water and exchanging gossip.

"You paid *how* much for a set of strings?"

"I can't tell you, but let's just say it was eye-watering..."

"So after that fiasco, were you asked to play in the next concert?"

"Sadly not..."

"And did the percussion player ever say sorry?"

"No, but he will..."

"How did you manage, when you found you'd forgotten your concert clothes?"

"Luckily we weren't too far from a certain well-known chain store and I had time to nip in and buy a black top and skirt – I managed to borrow a pair of black shoes from one of the ladies in the box office..."

"It's going to be a great concert," Holly said. "And it's so much fun out here, listening to everyone."

"Absolutely!" Allegra gave a wide grin. "I'm surprised how many of this bunch of people I've worked with before. It's our musical family."

"Seem to be a lot more arriving now," Holly commented.

"Yes, they must be the choir," Allegra said. "They're in the second piece in the concert."

"Mozart?"

"Yes. Mass in C. I've played it a few times," Allegra said. "You?"

"Yes, played it a couple of years ago in Vienna," Holly answered.

"He must be one of the solo singers," Allegra said, as a tall blonde creature swept past them, with a coat artfully draped over one shoulder to display its red silk lining.

"He looks like a Greek god," Holly said, completely enraptured by the vision.

"He does rather," Allegra agreed. "He'll set hearts aflutter in the choir, no doubt about it."

"Maybe the orchestra too," Holly murmured as they made their way back to the rehearsal.

Half an hour later, the concert hall was filled with pulsating music as the soloists, choir and orchestra all poured their hearts into Mozart's breathtaking melodies – then, disaster struck. Clutching at his chest, Maestro Rostopovsky called for some water and looked as if he were about to collapse. The Greek god singer rushed to his aid and in the nick of time caught the frail conductor before he hit the floor.

"Ah," the chorus cooed.

"What a hero," the bass player from Dubai asserted.

"Right place, right time," the flautist in purple said.

"Can we have some help here," the Greek god

singer shouted. "Is there a doctor here? Maybe one of the choir?"

"I'm a doctor," one of the altos called as she jumped down from the choir steps and rushed to help. "Here, let me...thank you for catching him...you've done a grand job...what did you say your name was?"

"Boris. Boris the bass. At your service."

"Ah," the choir cooed again. "Boris the bass."

"Maybe if everyone were to sit down?" Boris suggested. "Quiet, please. Let the doctor assess the patient..."

After a tense few minutes, it was decided the maestro had been overcome by overwork, heat and dehydration, but as a precaution, he had better be taken to hospital to be checked over.

"Is there a conductor in the choir," Boris asked, "or in the orchestra? Someone who could conduct the rest of the rehearsal? No? In that case, I will offer my humble self to help our musical forces in their hour of need."

Without further ado, he leapt onto the podium, raised his hands high above his head and yelled,

"Let's start from the next chorus, ladies and gentlemen. Look this way, breathe and..."

"He's not bad," Holly whispered to Allegra.

"Indeed he is not," she answered. "I wouldn't like to have to conduct this lot at short notice, would you? He's got courage."

At that precise moment, Boris turned to look at Allegra. He fixed her with a megawatt beaming smile, followed by a cheeky wink, and she felt hot and cold all over, lingering thoughts of Zack firmly squeezed out of her mind.

Later, back at the hotel in the room they were sharing, Holly and Allegra collapsed onto their beds, worn out by all the drama.

"It's been a long day," Holly said.

"Too right! Delayed flight, extra-long rehearsal..."

"Hope the maestro will be all right for tomorrow."

"He'll be fine," Allegra said. "Probably needs a rest and then he can take over again in the morning."

"Or maybe not," Holly said, looking at her phone.

"What do you mean?" Allegra asked.

"There's an email from the orchestral manager," Holly explained. "They've decided Maestro Rostopovsky shouldn't do the concert but must rest and restore himself."

"Is Boris going to conduct?"

"No, sadly not. He's needed as the bass soloist. They say they've been lucky to be able to get someone well-known who's agreed to fly over immediately from Switzerland..."

"No, not..." Allegra sat upright on her bed, her eyes wide with shock.

"Yes. Sorry, Allegra. He's flying over from Zurich as soon as possible – it's Zack. He's flying through the night to get here, to save the occasion."

Chapter 4

Pete Grapples With Retirement

"But who is Alice, Pete? Who is she?"

Cathy stared at herself in the long mirror in her bedroom, practising what she would say to her husband when she next saw him. This had been Maeve's advice, after Cathy had shared her discovery of Pete's unusual text from the mysterious Alice.

"You need to rehearse asking him who Alice is – make sure your expression is non-threatening, because it's all a huge mistake, you know it is, but you need to be clear and you have to know what on earth's going on," Maeve had said.

Cathy had closed her eyes for a brief moment on hearing this. The situation seemed completely unreal to her. What exactly was it she was supposed to be non-threatening about? What was it Maeve suspected Pete of doing? Surely she couldn't be suggesting Pete would be 'carrying on' with someone? Her Pete? The very idea was laughable. They'd been married for the best part of her adult life...and yet it was a strange message to find...but no, Cathy said firmly to herself. I'm not questioning Pete like this. It's ridiculous! I trust him implicitly. The poor man must have got himself into some sort of situation or muddle, like he did before, that'll be what's going on. The best thing is if I simply ask him.

"Hello love! I'm home. Fancy a cuppa?"

Pete's voice floated up the stairs and Cathy pulled herself together.

"Be down in a second," she called. "And yes, tea would be lovely."

Soon the pair of them were sitting outside relaxing in the autumn sunshine.

"Had a good time?" Cathy asked.

"Yes," Pete replied. "Popped into the library to change my books and I went to the information session about all the new adult education courses too."

"Oh yes. You said there was going to be a talk in the library when you were browsing on the computer a few days ago. Anything sound interesting?"

"Cooking," Pete said. "Thought you've been soldiering on in the kitchen all these years and I'd like to give you a break and have a go myself. What do you think?"

"I think it's a great idea," Cathy said. "When do you start?"

"Alice says I can start tomorrow," Pete replied.

"Alice?"

"She was giving the talk," Pete explained. "She's in charge of bookings for the courses. I messaged her a few days ago through the council website and she's been encouraging me to find out more about the sort of course I'd like to do."

"I'm thrilled!" Cathy jumped up and gave Pete a hug. "You have no idea how happy I am."

"What's going on," Pete said. "You're behaving oddly."

"Oh dear." Cathy hung her head. "You know me too well."

Pete scratched his ear and looked bewildered. "Cathy – what is it?"

Cathy cleared her throat. "I found a message from Alice on your phone yesterday, when I took your phone by accident, and I thought...I wondered...I didn't know what to think or wonder, to be honest..."

"Cathy!" Pete roared with laughter. "You know you're the only woman in the world for me. For ever."

"I know, I know," Cathy murmured as Pete gathered her into a bear-like hug. "It's so silly. I shouldn't even have looked at your phone, but I thought it was mine and Maeve said..."

"I might have known Maeve would be involved," Pete said. "I feel sorry for her, I do, with her over-active imagination. The woman watches so many melodramatic soaps and films, she sees intrigue everywhere and views everyone with suspicion – all with absolutely no good reason."

"Dear Maeve," Cathy said. "She's always looking for something exciting to think about. Everyday life must seem tame to her, after all those years running the school as Headmistress. She used to rule the place with an iron grip – though with a very tender heart too."

"Yes, I suppose she must miss all that, the everyday conflicts and situations she was so good at dealing with. Bet she runs the charity shop efficiently."

"She certainly does. There was a moth there last week, and within minutes, Maeve had tracked down the bag of clothes it had had the temerity to fly out of. She then traced the donor of the bag, rang her up and gave her quite an earful of advice down the phone."

"Advice or abuse?" Pete sniggered.

"Advice! Behave yourself, Pete."

"And what happened to the moth itself?" Pete asked. "No, don't tell me. You know how much I hate blood sports."

"In that case, I won't tell you its fate," Cathy said. "Let's just say it came to a sticky – but mercifully quick – end. But seriously, Maeve's always been keen to share her views."

"Don't I know it," Pete said thoughtfully. "She used to give us plenty of parenting advice when Allegra was small."

"Indeed she did," Cathy said, "although I have to admit some of it was very useful and she always meant well." Cathy sighed. "I remember Allegra told me that Maeve even tried to advise her about Zack, once they were engaged."

"But she wouldn't know anything about that," Pete said, "not being married or attached to anyone."

"Maybe that's why she felt no compunction about offering advice so freely," Cathy replied.

"What? Oh, I see what you mean. She wasn't held back by any sort of reference to reality or experience," Pete said.

"Exactly! Her romantic experiences have been exclusively informed by television and those novels she's always getting out of the library with the lurid covers."

"Ah, yes. The ones with a dagger and a heart on the front, perhaps with a pool of blood in the corner?" Pete suggested.

"Exactly."

"I used to confiscate those when I was teaching," Pete said, "if I saw them sticking out of a sixth former's bag."

"You book snob!"

"I gave them back at the end of the day," Pete reassured Cathy, "mainly because I didn't want them in my possession any longer than strictly necessary!"

"We get quite a lot of that sort of reading matter in the charity shop," Cathy mused. "Maeve puts the books on a high shelf."

"So only she can reach them?" Pete sniggered again.

"Poor Maeve," Cathy said. "I feel sorry for her now. She must be at a bit of a loose end sometimes, with no close family. I wish I could do something to help."

"You help her by volunteering at the charity shop – you even fill in when other people are absent too."

"Yes, it was a bit beyond the call of duty yesterday – but we had a lot of fun." Cathy smiled at her husband.

"In between suspecting me of goodness knows what."

"Point taken. Actually Pete, I didn't suspect you of anything untoward – of course I didn't – I was concerned though because I thought you might have got yourself in a muddle again. You remember when you first stopped work and started sorting everything out in the house, rearranging all my belongings too, putting my herbs and spice jars in alphabetical order, books in order of size, all neatly lined up in such a way I was scared to disturb the display by taking one out of the bookcase to read?"

"Yes, guilty as charged," Pete agreed.

"Then you started chucking stuff away? Loads of possessions, maybe some of them things we needed?"

"Yes, I do. That was hard work," Pete said, wiping his hand across his brow. "Feel tired just thinking about going up and down the ladder to the loft umpteen times a day."

"Luckily I managed to sneak a few prize pieces back," Cathy said. "And what about the shed – remember clearing the shed?"

"Certainly do! We found some real treasures. The hoard of rusty nails, the rolls of garden twine turning to green dust, the massive collection of plastic plant pots, impossible to recycle..."

"All of great value," Cathy said, "and destined for the dump. And after you'd got rid of that rubbish, you started buying up tons of items we didn't need on eBay."

Pete hung his head in mock shame, whispering "Sorry."

"No need to apologise. It was another step on your journey towards accepting retirement...and, I thought maybe..."

"Oh, I see," Pete said. "You thought perhaps I was behaving in a, how can I put it, slightly eccentric way again? The next phase along my journey of trying to find out what to do with the rest of my life?"

"Got it," Cathy said. "I thought Alice could have been part of your next hare-brained scheme, maybe an acupuncturist or a hang-gliding instructor, a teacher from a fitness boot camp or even one of those..."

"Steady on!" Pete laughed and swept Cathy into his arms. "So you approve of the cookery classes?"

"Definitely," Cathy replied. "I'll give you a list of my favourite dishes."

"No need," Pete said. "I know them all already and I used a spreadsheet on my phone to plan some meus while I was on the bus coming home. I'm going to start by learning to make a quiche."

"Ambitious, for someone who's not, how can I put it, *au fait* with the kitchen."

"Why do you think I'm going on the course?"

Pete's logic was impeccable and Cathy was pleased to see her husband looking enthusiastic. She'd been a little worried for some time that he wasn't enjoying his retirement as much as he should, and he had been through some rather annoying phases – who could forget the time he decided to get up at 5.30 every morning, to write his memoirs? Thank goodness that didn't last too long – it couldn't, as he became totally exhausted and succumbed to man flu.

"You'll have a great time at your new course," Cathy said. "Maybe I should look out a pinny for you?"

"I don't think men wear 'pinnies' in the kitchen," Pete said. "I thought I'd take my old boiler suit with me; it'll be just the ticket."

"It's covered in oil," Cathy protested, "and will be far too hot. I've got a better idea. I saw a chef's apron in the charity shop yesterday – I'll give Maeve a quick ring and see if it's still there."

"Ok," Pete said. "I'm going to have a look at my spread sheet again. The course starts on Thursday and I want to be ready."

As Cathy was about to call Maeve, she saw a text on her phone from Allegra.

Hi Mum! Our conductor's ill and Boris the bass, one of the soloists, has taken over rehearsals until the sub-

stitute arrives...the new conductor is Zack – he's arriving soon...

Chapter 5

Drama In Spain

"Hello everyone!" Zack strode onto the platform where the orchestra and choir were assembled. "It's terrific to be here."

He shook Boris's hand.

"Thanks for keeping the show on the road – I've heard you've been doing a great job. Now, we need to get on. From the top, everyone..."

He looks tired, Allegra thought. Black circles under his eyes. He's lost weight too, since we were together...

"Allegra!" Holly whispered urgently. "We're starting."

Allegra lifted her bow and allowed herself to forget everything, revelling in Mozart's glorious harmonies.

"Thank you, thank you," Zack said at the end of the piece. "I can see Boris has done a fine job keeping it all together."

Boris grinned and took a bow, waving madly to everyone.

"And now, maybe the singers could all leave as quietly as possible? I'll see you tonight at the concert. Meanwhile, orchestra, let's go straight into the Beethoven. We've got time for a quick run through before you all take a well-deserved break."

Allegra found it harder to concentrate in the Beethoven. As the dramatic chords rang out, she thought back to when everything had started to go wrong for her and Zack.

It had been shortly after they'd become engaged that Allegra had begun to wonder if she'd made the right choice. Zack had seemed to change, become quieter, almost moody on occasions.

He should have been happy, with so much to look forward to. Allegra couldn't understand it. Maybe they'd got engaged too soon – perhaps they hadn't known each other well enough?

It had been a whirlwind of a courtship, with both of them away so often, travelling with different orchestras, sometimes only meeting up for the briefest of times.

Once they were engaged, Zack had asked her to turn down some work which would have meant her travelling to the Far East for a few weeks, as he had a big concert coming up in New York and wanted her to be there to support him. Allegra had said no, she couldn't afford to turn the opportunity down – her career was important to her, surely he could understand? He'd accused her of not supporting him and they'd had their first real row.

The pair had made up almost immediately, both shocked by the angry harsh words they'd said to each other, and both resolving not to let such a thing happen again. They decided they should put some time aside to talk about how they would manage their careers, both involving so much touring – after all, once they were married, it would be crazy if they were hardly ever in the same country as each other. Zack had pointed out more than once that as an up-and-coming conductor, he would be able to recommend Allegra for work with whichever orchestra he was invited to conduct, but she wasn't happy with this idea. It would be convenient and help them achieve their aim of being able to spend more time together, for sure, but Allegra wanted to be offered jobs on merit, not merely through Zack.

"I haven't worked hard all these years just to give it up and trail after a man," she had said, surprising herself with the strength of her feelings.

"I'm not just 'a man'," Zack had replied. "I'm the person you say you want to spend the rest of your life with, or at least that's what you lead me to believe."

"Of course I do," Allegra replied. "Please don't doubt me, Zack – but I've always dreamt of a musical career; I'd like to try to sort out what form it's going to take after we're married."

Zak's answer was to snap, "It's hard enough trying to cope with everything – please don't make it harder."

Allegra wondered what he meant by this comment, but the moment passed before she could ask him to clarify what it was he was struggling to cope with. He seemed to be hinting at some sort of pre-existing burden but for the life of her, she couldn't think what it might be.

On another occasion, Zack had said that once they were married, and if they were lucky enough to have a family, he wanted Allegra to give up her playing career. Allegra was shocked to hear this – they hadn't discussed what they would do if and when children arrived. It might be that she would indeed retire from playing, at least for a number of years, but she wanted this to be something they discussed together, not something to be assumed, or, even worse, imposed on her.

These incidents were enough to give the couple a warning to pause before they tied the knot, but in the end, it wasn't disagreeing about the details of their future lives together that drove them apart, but something else entirely

Allegra was shaken out of her reverie by the fierce ending of Beethoven's Fifth Symphony.

"Magnificent!" Zack said. "I don't think you lot need a conductor at all. You're incredible! See you all this evening, seven o'clock sharp, backstage."

"You OK?" Holly asked Allegra. "I didn't feel you were really with me during the play through."

"Saving myself for this evening," Allegra replied. "Hey, look, isn't that Boris over there?"

"So it is," Holly said. "The singers didn't have to stay to hear the Beethoven – wonder why he did."

"Hello ladies," Boris said as he bounded up to

Holly and Allegra. "I'm collecting people to go out for a bite to eat before the performance – care to join us?"

"What a great idea!" Holly said. "How kind of you to ask."

"Yes, thank you," Allegra agreed. "Lovely. We need to leave our violins in the dressing room – shall we meet you outside in a few minutes?"

"I wouldn't leave anything valuable backstage," Boris advised. "Take your instruments with you."

"You're right; can't be too careful," Holly agreed.

"Goodness, I would be heartbroken if anything happened to my violin," Allegra added. "My poor parents practically had to take out a second mortgage to buy this for me when I was at college."

Allegra glanced over her shoulder to see if she could see Zack, but there was no sign of him.

"He left immediately," Holly whispered. "Stop thinking about him."

"I wasn't," Allegra replied. "Just checking because I don't want to run into him again by accident. I couldn't face it. Why would I ever want to see him again?"

"No reason." Holly rolled her eyes. "Come on. I'm starving."

Boris led Holly, Allegra and quite a few others from the orchestra to a popular and crowded restaurant nearby, where they found a jolly bunch from the choir already feasting on local delicacies at an enormously long wide table near the main doors.

"The restaurant management know we have to eat quickly, because of the concert," Boris explained, "so I've taken the liberty of ordering tapas. There's bound to be something you like; please, sit down and dig in."

There was quite a party atmosphere and Boris was definitely at the centre of it. As usual, with any group of musicians, viola jokes were shared freely, particularly by the viola players themselves.

"Oi, Boris! How do you get two viola players to play in tune with each other?"

"That's an old one!" Boris shouted down the table. "Ask one of them to leave, obviously."

"What about this one – why do you think viola players don't play hide and seek?"

"I don't know," Holly said. "Why don't viola players play hide and seek?"

"Oh, I know this," Allegra said with a smile. "Because no one would look for them."

"Excellent!" Boris cackled. "And now the last one, as we need to leave soon to go and get changed for the concert. How do you keep a violin from being stolen? Anybody? No? Put it in a viola case. Get it? Viola case...hey, what's the matter Allegra?"

"My violin! It was here, beside me. Where's it gone? It must have been stolen!"

"Hilarious!" Boris yelled, slapping his thighs and hooting with mirth. "You nearly had me there...hey, hang on, you're not joking are you? Sweetie, please don't cry, here, take my handkerchief..."

"I can't have lost it," Allegra sobbed. "It means everything to me. Oh, please would you all mind looking around – maybe it's been moved? Can anyone see it?"

Boris clicked his fingers. "May we have some help here? Call the police, or something? Look at the CCTV, if you have any?"

"Of course *señor*, so sorry *señor*; I'm sure we can have this cleared up in a moment." The restaurant manager rushed over to the table and tried his best to help, calling the police when it became obvious the violin had well and truly vanished.

"What will you play on this evening if your violin doesn't turn up in time?" Holly asked.

"No idea," Allegra said, "and I can't see it turning up within the next thirty minutes, so I've a real problem."

"Don't worry," Boris reassured her. "I have my violin with me, back in my hotel room. You can borrow it for as long as you need to."

"But you're a singer," Holly said, astounded.

"I play the violin too," Boris replied. "Badly, I admit it, but I always take it on tour and practise when I can."

Allegra too looked amazed.

"I know you're thinking of all the jokes about singers," Boris said. "How singers have nothing but resonance between their ears, but I promise you I have quite a decent violin in my hotel room and I'm going to rush away and get it. It's the least I can do, after encouraging you to bring your violin to the restaurant."

Allegra, before she could help herself, leant forward and gave Boris a peck on the cheek out of gratitude, at the very moment that Zack walked into the restaurant accompanied by two policemen.

"I heard what's being going on," he said, "and thought I'd better come and see if I could help."

Allegra blushed scarlet as she realised Zack must have seen her kiss Boris.

But why should that matter? It's not as if Zack has any interest in me and besides, I can do what I like, she thought. He's with Vanessa now, his fiancée, and I don't care at all. Couldn't be less interested in the man.

"May we ask you a few questions, madam," one of the policemen said to Allegra, "to help with our enquiries?"

"Of course."

"Are there any identifying marks on the violin or the bow? Anything else in the case to help us identify the stolen property?"

"I've got pictures of the violin on my phone," Allegra said, "showing the various markings and so on; there are a lot of distinguishing features because it's an old, well-used instrument – the same goes for the bow. As for the case, I've got the usual spare strings and rosin in there. My initials are engraved on the handle. That will help? Oh, and I had a spare bow in there too. Nothing fancy, but I always carry a spare."

Allegra's heart beat faster as she decided not to mention the special, favourite photographs she had, tucked safely down the side of the velvet lining; she couldn't mention them, not with Zack standing there, her Zack, her beautiful Zack, lost to her forever. How could she ever say that the photos she carried with her everywhere in the world and looked at on countless occasions, kissed even, were none other than two tiny dog-eared snaps from a photo booth of her and Zack, taken on a day trip to the seaside? She could see the photos now, imprinted in her mind and heart forever, the two of them happy and carefree, Zack's hand resting lightly on her shoulder, both smiling at each other, so much in love. The photos meant more to her than anything in the world, showing a time when they'd had their whole future ahead of them – before she'd ruined it.

Chapter 6

Pete Cooks A Quiche

"Sure is an eventful trip," Pete said, a few days later. "At least the first concert went smoothly, after all the trouble."

"Yes, but poor Allegra – she's still frantically worried about her violin," Cathy said. "The Spanish police don't seem to have made much headway with finding it yet, and it'll be much more difficult for her to find out how the police are doing once she's back in London."

"She'll be back by tonight, won't she?" Pete asked.

"Yes. Not quite sure what time."

"Don't worry, love," Pete said. "I'm sure the police are doing their best and Allegra can borrow the violin from this Boris chap as long as need be, apparently."

"I know." Cathy sighed. "And the violin is insured, but that's not the point. The instrument means so much to Allegra – she's played on it since she was at college. Do you remember when she played 'The Lark Ascending' for the first time?"

Cathy felt her eyes misting over as the vision of

her precious teenaged daughter conjuring a beautiful melody out of her violin, swaying in time to the music, popped into her mind.

"The performance was a triumph," Pete agreed, "but we still have our memories and of course our lovely daughter. There's not much we can do except trust the Spanish police and their investigation."

"Shame there wasn't CCTV," Cathy commented.

"They don't have CCTV everywhere." Pete smirked. "Maybe it's not only Maeve who watches too many television dramas!"

Cathy grinned. "We'll have to wait and trust the police, as you say."

She grabbed a tea towel and started to clear the draining board. "This Boris sounds a pleasant sort of person."

"Cathy! No matchmaking. It's none of our business."

"I'm not matchmaking – simply making an observation. He must think something of Allegra if he's prepared to lend her his violin."

"And to be fair, she did say she admired his conducting and the way he took charge when Rostopovsky was taken ill." Pete took a large ceramic dish out of the kitchen cupboard and stared into it carefully.

"Yes, indeed. Wasn't it great Rostopovsky was able to come to the concert, to sit in the audience?" Cathy said. "Pete? What *are* you doing?"

"I'm doing my homework," Pete said as he

opened the fridge door and pulled out some cheese and bacon.

"Oh, how could I forget?" Cathy smiled. "It's quiche day, isn't it? I'm glad you're enjoying your cookery course."

"I had a great time at the first class yesterday. And the new apron went down a treat. Our tutor said I looked very professional. Glad you persuaded me not to wear my old boiler suit – it would've looked a little out of place."

"Glad you followed my advice." Cathy chuckled and leant over to kiss Pete gently on the cheek. "I'll be off now. I need to pop in to see Mrs Oatcake."

"Mrs Oatcake? Who's that?"

"She's one of the ladies I visit, taking library books round – didn't I mention her before?"

Pete looked blank. "Can't keep up with your good deeds," he said. "I have a vague memory you said you were considering joining the volunteer library home reading scheme, but I wasn't completely sure what it involved and I certainly didn't know you'd started."

"I joined the scheme some time ago," Cathy said. "I've visited Mrs Oatcake a few times now – she's not been at all well and requested home library visits."

"How's it going?"

Cathy cleared her throat before replying, "I'm sure I'll manage to find some books she enjoys, given time."

"That well?" Pete hacked some bacon into rough

stringy pieces. "What are you doing after you've visited her?"

"Church flowers, followed by a hair appointment."

"Oh yes, you're trying the new place on the high street, aren't you?" Pete picked up a bit of bacon from the floor and added it to the pile of ingredients for the quiche filling.

"I am."

"What was it called again?"

"You know perfectly well what it's called, Pete."

"Humour me."

"'Jane Hair'. It's not that funny!"

"Yes, it is," Pete said, wiping tears from his eyes. "And is it a trim you're having, or are you perhaps having some Wuthering Highlights?"

Pete was doubled up now, overcome with mirth.

"OK," Cathy said. "Wuthering Highlights *is* quite funny."

"Plenty more where that came from. Reminds me of when I used to sit in the staff room at break with my colleagues, all making up the most terrible puns, mostly about the set works we were teaching the kids. I remember..."

"Enough," Cathy said. "I'm not in the mood. I'm still worried about Allegra."

"In what way?"

"I'm concerned she hasn't said anything about Zack."

"Good news, isn't it?" Pete grated some cheese vigorously, holding his fingers perilously close to the sharp metal spikes.

"Not necessarily. I know her. If she didn't mind seeing him again, working with him, I think she'd have said. It's the silence I find suspicious. I do hope she's not been upset by seeing him again."

"You're worried because she *hasn't* said she's upset? Ouch, my fingers. Surely if she was upset, she would've told you?" Pete frowned as he started to cut an onion into large irregular chunks.

"It's a feeling I've got...can't explain..."

Pete shook his head and carried on chopping.

"I'm worried, but not about Allegra. I'm worried by the amount of chores you're doing for other people," he remarked.

"I like to keep busy!"

"Mmm. I suppose as long as you're enjoying it, there's no harm. And now I've got my cookery course, I'm incredibly busy again. I haven't got time to miss my teaching, no, not at all!"

"You loved teaching, we both did, but there comes a time..." Cathy's voice tailed off into an uncertain silence. What sort of time was she having now? Maybe she was remembering her work with the rosy tinted glow of hindsight, but nowadays, she seemed to be even more at everyone's beck and call than she'd been when in charge of her Reception Class. What's more, she suspected that some of the characters she had to deal with in her retirement were slightly less well-behaved and mature than some of the little people she'd been in charge of at school.

"Crumbs!" she said, glancing up at the kitchen clock. "I'd better get my skates on. See you later. Already looking forward to the quiche!"

"It's not difficult, this cooking lark, is it, once you get going? I've already made the filling, well, most of it – pastry next." Pete patted the bag of flour in front of him on the table.

"Should those eggs be in the filling?" Cathy pointed at three eggs still in their shells, rolling around precariously on the counter.

"Ah yes. Thank you. Wouldn't have tasted the same without those little beauties!"

"See you later."

On her way to Mrs Oatcake, Cathy's phone rang.

"Hope she's not cancelling," she said, diving into her handbag. "Oh! Hello Pete!"

"I'm worried," Pete said. "Very worried. I don't think pastry is easy to make, no, not at all. It's so sticky and grey. Doesn't look right."

"Don't worry," Cathy soothed. "See if you can roll it out."

"Roll it out?"

"With the rolling pin."

"Oh yes. The tutor said something about a rolling pin. Do we have one?"

"Bottom of the cupboard in the dresser, right hand side. Got to go, Pete. I'm nearly at Mrs Oatcake's."

"Thanks love. Appreciate your help..."

No sooner was Cathy comfortably seated in an

arm chair in Mrs Oatcake's sitting room, sipping tea, than her phone went off again.

"Not important," she said after a hasty glance at the screen. "My husband. Now, where were we?"

"I was explaining to you what sort of books I thought I would enjoy," Mrs Oatcake said, "before your husband interrupted us."

"Sorry, better take this," Cathy said. "It's my husband again. Hello? You can't manage to use the rolling pin?"

Mrs Oatcake flicked her eyes heavenwards and smirked.

"So you've squidged it into the dish with your fingers and you want to know if I think it'll work?"

Mrs Oatcake shook her head.

"It might..." Cathy said, shrugging. "Yes, I think you're correct, it might spread out a bit during the cooking process. Yes, your tutor is right when she told you cooking is a mysterious process..."

"Chemistry with a dash of magic," Mrs Oatcake added helpfully.

"Yes, indeed, did you hear that, Pete? Mrs Oatcake says cooking is chemistry with a dash of...ah, you heard...And yes, it's also true some things don't look too good until they're cooked but you can be pleasantly surprised once they come out of the oven – like scones, exactly...'Bye Pete. Many apologies, Mrs Oatcake. Do go on. You were telling me which authors you admire..."

As Cathy left Mrs Oatcake's house, on her way to

tackle the church flowers, she rang Pete to check on the progress of the quiche.

"You had to start again? Why?"

"I hadn't quite finished making the filling. You remember when you saw the eggs on the side? Still in their shells? I wasn't sure what to do with them or how many to use. I noticed the pot of cream on the counter too. I'd forgotten to add some. I *think* I'd forgotten – to be honest, I wasn't sure. And I didn't know if I should add some seasoning."

"But I still don't understand why you had to start again. Why couldn't you look at the recipe? Wait a minute please Pete, would you? I'm getting on the bus...OK. Sitting down now. Fire away."

"The recipe was inside the dish, printed on the china, and I'd covered it with pastry. I tried to peel the pastry sheet back, but because it wasn't a sheet, more of a cobbled-together lumpy mess, once I had the stuff in my hands, it sort of slipped through my fingers in a gungy way and fell on the floor. Our tutor told us not to use ingredients that had been on the floor."

Cathy wisely decided not to mention that earlier, when they'd been in the kitchen together at home, she'd noticed Pete pick up a piece of bacon he'd dropped on the floor and add it to the filling. It wouldn't have been helpful, she felt. Under the circumstances.

"Poor you," she said. "But what a great idea, to start again, but to photograph the recipe inside the dish on your phone before you lined it with fresh pastry...hang on, I've got to get off here...what did you say?"

"I couldn't read the recipe on my phone because it was too small – should have worn my reading glasses – and when I tried to enlarge it, I deleted it."

"If I were you," Cathy said, in the kindly, patient tone she'd previously reserved for talking to five year olds in the classroom, "I'd look up another recipe, on the internet. See if you can find one using roughly the same ingredients."

"Thanks. I was sure you'd know what to do."

Pete rang off and Cathy hurried into the church to begin sorting and snipping, helping to create lovely floral displays to gladden the hearts of the congregation.

It was only later, when she was halfway through her pampering session in 'Jane Hair' – the junior was raking conditioner through Cathy's thick locks with her red talons, in an attempt to give her a relaxing scalp massage – that she realised Pete must have been successful in his cooking. There had been no more desperate phone calls – surely a good sign

Cathy felt all was well with the world as she left the salon, her lustrous curls bouncing around her shoulders. Mrs Oatcake seemed to have enjoyed her visit, the flower arranging at the church had gone smoothly, Pete would have the meal ready by the time she got home – and she felt like a million dollars with her new hair-do. She didn't have to wait long for the bus and was home within minutes.

"Hello!" she called. "I'm back...eek! What's that smell?"

Cathy flew straight to the kitchen and flung open the window to let the stench of charcoal escape.

"What's been going on? Arg! I stepped in something sticky on the floor. What is it?"

"Pastry. My first attempt. I tried to clear it up with a cloth but I might have missed a bit." Pete pointed to a tea towel lying on the side, encrusted with grey dry lumps.

"But what's the burning smell?"

"The second attempt."

"Oh Pete! What happened?"

"I forgot to set the timer. You know the book I've been wanting to finish for ages? The one about Egypt? I thought I'd read a bit of it while the quiche was cooking, but no sooner was I visiting the pyramids of Giza, dreaming of the far distant days of the great Pharaohs, than I fell fast asleep on the sofa. The smoke alarm woke me in the end. As I said, I should have set the timer. I know that now."

"Never mind. Accidents happen."

Cathy tried hard not to giggle as Pete walked across the floor and retrieved a crisp, black object from the bin, about the size of a thick dinner plate. "Here's the quiche," he said solemnly. "It's burnt."

"No kidding." Cathy burst out laughing. "Oh, sorry Pete, but you have to see the funny side!"

Pete's face creased into a delightful smile as he

lobbed the ruined quiche back into the swing-top bin.

"So Cathy, do you fancy going out for supper?"

Chapter 7

Return To England

"Are you sure you didn't make a mistake, Allegra? About the engagement ring?" Holly held on firmly to the handle as the taxi swung round a corner at speed.

"No mistake. Vanessa was wearing Zack's grandmother's ring. I should be able to recognise it, if anyone can." Allegra slumped in her seat.

The tour had been a triumph and now they were on their way to the airport to fly back to England. Maestro Rostopovsky had been to all three concerts the orchestra and choir had performed, but as a member of the audience. He was well on the mend after his funny turn during the first rehearsal, but the medics had thought it best for him not to over-exert himself. The general opinion was that he'd been working far too hard – as usual. He'd been on one whistle stop tour after another, conducting and rehearsing all over the globe, and he was now off on a luxury cruise to take a well-deserved break.

Zack's reputation as a conductor was even better than before, after stepping into the breach so ably.

He'd been in all the newspapers, being praised to the skies.

"You'd think Zack would be getting quite big-headed with all these fantastic reviews," Holly said, scanning the newspaper, "except it's not his style."

"No," Allegra agreed. "I could say a lot of things about Zack, but I would never accuse him of being boastful or showing off."

"Sorry," Holly said. "Didn't mean to mention his name."

"Unavoidable in this case," Allegra replied. "He's been amazing, with the orchestra. But it changes nothing between us. He's still engaged to Vanessa."

"Do you mind?" Holly asked. "About Vanessa? I mean, you never said why you broke off your engagement, even to me, your best friend."

Allegra fiddled with the strap of her handbag.

"He started looking for someone – oh, I shouldn't say because he asked me not to, but heaven knows, after all this time, I can't see what harm it could do..."

"No," Holly said, "don't break a confidence – you'll regret it. But, whatever it was, do you think you made the right decision?"

"I thought so at the time," Allegra said, "because he wasn't ready to commit. There was too much else from his past he needed to sort out. But now," she continued, in a whisper so soft that Holly had to lean forward to catch her words, "I suspect if I'd acted in a more mature way, maybe I could have helped him. I shouldn't have left him to deal with it on his own..."

"Here we are ladies," interrupted the taxi driver. *"Aeropuerto*! Now you fly back to England and your beloved rain."

Holly laughed as she paid the driver.

"We don't love the rain," she said. "We get used to it! Thank you, yes, you too and goodbye."

"We need to run," Allegra said. "We'll be late – come on Holly!"

"There's plenty of time."

"No, we need to get going," Allegra urged, rushing forward, with the wheels of her case spinning madly as she ran into the terminal.

She could see Zack jumping out of a nearby taxi.

"Coming," Holly panted as she raced after her friend, "though I don't know what the fuss is ..."

Holly caught up with Allegra at the check-in desk.

"You don't need to be frightened of Zack, do you? You've been with him all week."

"But that was mostly in a crowd," Allegra qualified.

She wasn't ready to have any sort of personal conversation with Zack. Besides, the airport was reminding her of Zack's new fiancée, Vanessa. The ruby ring had looked gorgeous on her finger. Her hands were shapely and elegant, with beautifully manicured long, very long, nails. Hang on; she couldn't be a musician, could she, with extravagant nails? Zack always said he loved Allegra even more because of their shared passion for music. She was sure he'd only be interested in a musician. He could have changed of course, or Vanessa must be a singer, that would be it. Singers often had lovely long nails, not needing their fingers to fly nimbly over an instrument.

But Zack often used to make jokes about singers, Allegra reminded herself, recalling his favourite.

"How do you know when a soprano is at your door? She can't find the key and doesn't know when to come in."

Allegra felt a giggle bubbling up, a giggle she hastily subdued as she realised Zack was right behind them in the queue.

"Flying back to England?" Holly asked.

"Yes," Zack replied.

His voice, his beautiful, silky, deep, gravelly voice. Allegra breathed slowly then forced herself to turn round and greet him.

"Hi!"

"Hi," Zack said.

His eyes. Meltingly attractive, velvety chocolate brown with a gorgeous tinge of dark green...

"Did you pack this bag yourself?" the check-in assistant asked Allegra. "Any knives? Sharp objects?"

Only Cupid's arrow, piercing my heart again. That must count as a sharp object, surely?

Of all the coincidences, Zack happened to have been allocated the seat on the plane next to Allegra. He had the window seat, with Allegra in the middle and Holly on the aisle. Allegra thought about trying to manoeuvre Holly to sit in the middle, but instead decided to embrace her fate.

"Enjoy the concerts?" Zack asked.

"Yes."

"Where are you working next?" Zack tried.

"London."

"How have you been?"

"Look – we're taking off! I love this bit." Allegra stared across Zack and saw the yellow and brown ground disappearing, the sun beating down and reflecting off the airport rooves.

"Have to get used to an English autumn again," Holly said. "Rain, as the taxi driver kindly reminded us."

There followed a polite conversation between the three of them about the weather before Holly started flicking through a magazine and Allegra pulled out her Kindle.

"You haven't turned the page," Zack said to Allegra after a while. "How do you turn the page on a Kindle, anyway?"

Allegra showed him the button on the side, wondering why he'd been scrutinising her.

"Maybe it was a very interesting page and I was reading it several times over," she suggested.

"Unlikely, but possible." Zack smiled. "Tell me, I want to know, how have you been? How's your work going and how are your parents?"

"All fine, thank you. I know how your work's

been going because I've read about you in the papers. You're quite famous now! I'm so pleased for you."

Zack looked down at his hands. "Thank you."

Allegra decided to be bold. Where was the harm? It's not as if he could run away or scream at her.

"I'm pleased to see your personal life's good too."

"My what?"

"Vanessa? Your fiancée."

Zack laughed to hear this. He threw his head back hard against the seat, causing the lady directly behind him to say, "Steady, that's my coffee you're spilling!" which made him laugh even more. Finally, he wiped the tears from his eyes with a handkerchief embroidered with crotchets and quavers, causing Allegra to give a sudden gasp of recognition, and said,

"Allegra! I'm not engaged to Vanessa or anyone else, either. Whatever gave you that idea?"

"The ring," she said. "Your grandmother's ring."

"Ah." Zack inspected his nails. "You noticed the ring. After you, we, I mean..."

"After I threw the ring back at you and broke our engagement," Allegra said.

After I made the most stupid idiotic mistake of my life, one I'll regret until my dying day.

"Yes. Our broken engagement." Zack looked out of the window.

"So why was she wearing it?" Allegra demanded.

"My grandmother gave me the ring, as her elder grandson, to give to my intended wife, but after you, we, split up, I didn't want to have the ring any-more – I couldn't imagine giving it to anyone else, not after you...I talked to my grandmother and she thought it would be best to give it to Joe."

"Your brother Joe? Ah, Vanessa must be..."

"Vanessa's engaged to my brother Joe, correct. They're planning a spring wedding. We were on our way to join Joe in Switzerland for a few days' holiday when you saw us, although not a complete holiday for me; you know what I'm like – I took some music with me, hoping to get time to study a new piece I'm conducting soon."

Zack hasn't changed, Allegra thought. He was never without his precious music case, bulging with masterpieces.

"My brother Joe had gone out ahead of Vanessa and me," Zack continued, "because of some busi-ness he had there, and when you saw me with Vanessa, we were travelling out to join him at a lodge in the mountains. The three of us intended to spend a few days hiking."

"But you called her 'honey'."

Allegra still couldn't quite accept Zack's version of events – it was so very different from the painful narrative she'd spun in her mind, torturing herself with jealous thoughts. She also seriously doubted whether the glamorous creature she'd seen with Zack would have been tempted to go hiking, but appearances could be deceptive, as she was finding out.

"Honey? What? Oh, yes, I believe I did. Yes,

I definitely called Vanessa 'Honey'. And did you think...oh dear!"

Zack started laughing again.

"Vanessa's an actress and singer and has recently been in a Broadway show – in which she played the part of a young woman called Honey. Joe and her friends keep calling her Honey and it's become a bit of a joke – I've been calling her Honey too. No doubt we'll be calling her Christine soon because she's..."

"...going to be in 'Phantom of the Opera'! Gotcha!"

Relief flooded through Allegra and she squeezed her coffee cup so hard the brittle plastic crackled and split in her grasp.

"You always did have strong hands," Zack remarked. "Lucky you'd finished your coffee!"

Vanessa wasn't engaged to Zack – he was still single. She wasn't even his girlfriend, but was going to be his sister-in-law.

"I'm going to the ladies," Holly interrupted, as she undid her seat belt.

"I'll come with you!" Allegra said.

As the two friends queued in the narrow aisle, Allegra whispered,

"He's still got the handkerchief – the one with crotchets and quavers."

"The one you embroidered for him?" Holly asked.

"Yes!" Allegra's face split into a broad grin.

"I couldn't help overhearing," Holly said. "He's

not engaged – welcome news?"

"Absolutely!"

"Absolutely what?" a rich bass voice intoned behind Allegra.

"Boris!" she said with a start. "You gave me a fright creeping up on me! I didn't even know you were on the flight."

"And yet here I am," he said. Leaning forward, he gave Allegra a massive hug. "Sorry, I'm too broad to reach over to you, Holly," he apologised. "They couldn't make these aisles narrower if they tried."

"I'll forgive you this time, Boris!" Holly promised.

Boris pursed his lips and blew Holly a gentle kiss.

"Lovely to see you two ladies. I say, don't suppose either of you are free next Wednesday are you? I've got spare tickets for Covent Garden looking for a good home, and I'd be honoured if you could both join me."

"Sounds fun," Holly enthused. "Here, give me your number and we can get in touch."

"Yes, lovely." Allegra nodded. "Thank you."

"Super! Can't wait," Boris said.

Allegra remembered when she'd been to see 'Carmen' with Zack – he adored Covent Garden and one of his greatest ambitions was to conduct an opera there. She looked down the aisle towards their seats. Zack was standing up, staring at her. Was it her imagination, or was he glowering? Oh no – perhaps he'd seen Boris's rather over-enthusiastic embrace, then put two and two together and made five? Just as she'd thought they were getting on so well together...

Chapter 8

Sunday Lunch

"Did you put any water with those veg," Cathy asked, "before you put the saucepan on a high heat?"

"Of course," Pete answered. "I'm insulted that you think I didn't! I only put a tiny bit, mind you, because my tutor said it's much better to gently steam the veg. It keeps the vitamins and nutrients intact."

Cathy's eyebrows shot up, practically into her hair.

"What?" Pete asked. "Why are you checking up on me?"

Cathy rolled her eyes at the saucepan which was almost jumping off the hob, it was so hot. There was a hissing noise and steam was whooshing out, lifting the lid as it escaped.

"Ah. Maybe a bit more water?" Pete rushed the pan to the sink and gave it a quick blast of water from the tap. Pieces of singed broccoli and shredded, pale yellow carrot floated miserably to the surface, bobbing about in an accusatory sort of way.

"Water pressure's high today," Pete remarked. "I meant to put a tiny dribble of water in but..."

"Never mind," Cathy said. "You put the veg on very early." She looked at Pete's expression and added quickly, "In my humble opinion."

"No, you're right," Pete said. "My cookery teacher said it's best to wait until your guests arrive before starting. She told us a few amusing tales about how people used to put the Christmas veg on in November, to get her point across. Shame I didn't remember before I lit the gas."

"Nothing to worry about," Cathy said, "because we've got time to cook some more. Plenty left – bottom of the fridge in the cooler drawer."

Pete grabbed a tea towel and twisted it, as if trying to strangle a thought.

He might be mulling over the quiche episode, Cathy thought. Quichegate...I mustn't laugh, I mustn't...

At length Pete mumbled, "I'm beginning to think cooking's not my thing."

Cathy tried desperately to think of something encouraging to say while the clock ticked noisily in the background.

"Have you thought of joining a book group?" she said eventually. It sounded pretty lame, even to her ears.

Pete gave a lop-sided grin. "I prefer reading to cooking, for sure, but I want to do something in a group, not indulge in a solitary occupation like reading. Couldn't do that all the time – it'd drive me nuts! That's why I miss teaching – I long for the fun of the classroom, the kids, the banter, hearing them screaming for joy at break time and seeing their bright faces glowing with pleasure when you explain something to them and they suddenly get it."

"But you don't miss the marking, the record keeping, the endless meetings and so on, do you?" Cathy asked gently.

"I do not!" Pete shuddered. "It was a huge responsibility, being Head of English at Byron High School. No way would I want to go back to that. Thanks for reminding me why I left! Maybe cooking's not so bad. At least it's better than golf."

Cathy's shoulders went down a notch. She knew Pete was finding retirement challenging, but was relieved he had no plans to go back to teaching. He had found the last few years of his career incredibly stressful and she had zero desire to see him that unhappy and tired again. No, going back to teaching wouldn't be the right thing at all – for him.

Pete grinned. "Come on then. Want to help me peel some more carrots?"

Their first guest arrived soon afterwards. It was Allegra, back from her trip to Barcelona and longing to see her parents. She had time for a flying twenty-four hour visit, going down for Sunday lunch and planning to return on Monday to the flat she shared with Holly in south London.

"Good drive down darling?" Cathy asked as she folded Allegra in her warm embrace.

Poor lamb, she thought privately. She's thinner than ever and I don't like the way she looks so drawn. What's been going on? I do hope Zack hasn't been upsetting her again.

"All fine, Mum. Hi Dad! Great to see you. Something smells delicious. Roast lamb, isn't it? Is that your doing, Dad? I've been hearing all about your new course from Mum. You'll be setting up a restaurant chain soon!"

"Ah," Pete said, "Your mother's been helping me. I'll tell you the story of the vegetables later. Let's go and sit down shall we, while we wait for our other guest?"

"I hope you don't mind, dear," Cathy said, "but I asked Maeve to join us."

"Why should I mind?" Allegra answered. "I always enjoy seeing her, although sometimes I feel as if I'm back at school! I still think of her as Mrs Turnbull, not Maeve."

Cathy laughed. Maeve had taught at the same school as Cathy, which was how the two had met and become firm friends, and the friendship had continued even when Maeve had been appointed headmistress. Cathy often thought Maeve was like an unofficial godmother to Allegra. With no children of her own, she had taken a very strong interest in Allegra's welfare.

Half an hour later, Pete, Cathy, Allegra and Maeve

were tucking into a delicious roast dinner.

"Mum!" Allegra sighed with pleasure. "This is perfect! But I'm not sure I'll have room for pudding."

"Superb," Maeve commented, "as always! How do you get the roast potatoes to be so fluffy?"

"Pete advised me on those," Cathy replied. "A top tip from his cookery lesson."

"Ah yes," Maeve said. "I've yet to hear all the details about this course."

Pudding was a massive apple crumble, served with whipped cream.

"Or you can have yoghurt," Cathy said. "Maeve?"

Maeve shrieked with laughter. "Are you suggesting I should have yoghurt because it's low calorie?" she said. "Bit late, after everything else I've scoffed today! No, Allegra, of course I'm not offended by what your mother said. I think it's hilarious!"

Cathy looked at Maeve as she shook with mirth and felt a sudden rush of affection for her friend. Maeve could be tactless but she never took offence.

"Cream," Maeve said, "Definitely cream! And you, Allegra, you must have cream, lashings of it. Come on now, you're looking a bit peaky – get some meat on your bones, girl!"

Maeve reached across the table and spooned a more than generous helping of cream onto Allegra's apple pie.

"Mrs Turnbull!" Allegra protested. "I mean, Maeve! No! I simply haven't got room."

"And now you can tell me all about your trip

to Barcelona," Maeve said, leaning forward eagerly. "Spill the beans! What was it like meeting Zack after all this time?"

"Mum!" Allegra said. "I can't believe you've been talking..."

"Nonsense, my dear," Maeve said. "I follow the news, don't I? It was in the paper, how Zack saved the show by stepping in at the last minute. Quite a career opportunity!"

"I don't think he saw it as a career opportunity," Allegra said. "More a way he could help out."

"Nonsense," Maeve retorted. "Of course he had an eye on the main chance – he'd be a fool not to. And who's this Boris person the news referred to? Boris the bass?"

"He's the singer who took over," Allegra explained. "He's very charming. Larger than life personality and amazingly kind – fabulous voice and not bad at conducting either."

"He lent Allegra his violin," Cathy said, anxious to steer the conversation away from Zack. "Remember I mentioned it'd been stolen?"

"No result yet from the police," Pete added.

"Shocking! They can't be as efficient as our police here," Maeve said. "When my purse was stolen last year, taken from my bag by some sort of low life, in broad daylight too, it was found in the road and given in by a good Samaritan."

"Yes, with all your cards and money still there," Pete said. "I wondered at the time if perhaps you'd merely dropped your purse..."

Maeve raised her hands up in a cactus pose as if receiving a sudden electric shock.

"I'd never be so careless," she said. "It was *stolen* – beyond dispute."

Cathy smothered a smile. Maeve was completely impossible at times, but she was a dear friend. She'd been a listening ear for Cathy when Allegra had broken up with Zack in what had seemed to Cathy and Pete such an unexpected way. They'd been looking forward to welcoming Zack into their family and found the breakup both shocking and incomprehensible in equal measure. No point in raking up the past though, was there? What's done was done and hopefully it wouldn't be too long before Allegra found someone else, someone she could care for as deeply.

"This Boris," Maeve said to Allegra, "tell me more about him."

"I'm seeing him next week, actually," Allegra said. "He's taking Holly and me to the opera, to Covent Garden, on Wednesday. He's got a friend in the chorus there, a tenor, and he managed to get three tickets for the first night of 'The Barber of Seville'."

"Super," Cathy said.

"And I saw you winking at Mum, Maeve!" Allegra said. "Boris and I are friends, nothing more, although I wouldn't be surprised if Boris wasn't a bit keen on Holly, truth be told."

The corners of Mauve's mouth turned down a little as she digested this, but she soon recovered.

"What about his friend, the tenor?" she demanded.

Dear Maeve, Cathy thought. She simply never gives up! I feel the same – of course I'd like to see Allegra settled – but interfering isn't the way. I might have to have a word with Maeve next time we're alone. We're due to have one of our special days out in London next Tuesday – that might be a good occasion to have a heart to heart with her.

Every so often, Cathy and Maeve caught an early train from Bath up to Paddington and spent the day together looking at art galleries and hitting the shops, sometimes managing to catch a matinée at a West End theatre. It was a very welcome break for Cathy from her usual round of duties and she was thoroughly looking forward to it.

"Coffee?" Pete suggested. "Something I'm good at preparing. No, you ladies sit still while I clear the table. I'll load up the dishwasher and bring your coffee through. Relax!"

"You've got a good one there," Maeve said as soon as Pete had left the room.

"Not what you said last week," Cathy said, "when you told me to tackle him about the mysterious text."

"What's this?" Allegra asked.

"Nothing at all," Maeve said. "I made a silly snap judgement and your mother quite rightly told me what I was suspecting was laughable, but she was worried in a different way because as you know your father...oh, me and my big mouth, I always make things worse..."

Cathy explained to Allegra about the text from the lady at the library in charge of adult education, then reminisced about Pete's retirement phases and soon the three of them were chortling away at the absurdity of it all.

Pete staggered in with a tray of coffee and joined in the merriment by recounting the tale of his cooking disasters.

"And the quiche wasn't even recognisable," he said. "It was a solid black disc, like a Frisbee...and as for the veg this morning, words fail me..."

"Enough, Pete," Maeve begged. "I can't stop giggling...it's so funny."

"It's going to be almost impossible to clean the saucepan," Pete said. "I've left it to soak, but I don't hold out much hope."

"You have to stop laughing," Cathy said to Maeve, "because I think I can hear the house phone. Don't worry, I'll get it; stay there Pete and enjoy your coffee."

Cathy rushed out to the hall.

"It's for you, Allegra," she said a minute later, popping her head back round the door. "A call from London."

Cathy closed the door of the dining room as Allegra took her call in the hall.

"Is it Boris?" Maeve asked.

"No," Cathy said.

"Shame. He could have been ringing to ask Allegra out to dinner with Holly and his tenor friend..."

"Don't get carried away, Maeve," Pete said, smiling. "Who is it, love? You've gone rather quiet."

"It's Zack," Cathy said. "He said he wanted to talk to Allegra about something important."

Maeve twisted her napkin in her fingers and Pete looked down at the table cloth. As the room fell silent, they could hear Allegra's soft tones though the door saying,

"Yes, all right, Zack. Tomorrow it is. Six o'clock. Thank you."

Chapter 9

Back To London

Allegra was aiming to reach her flat in Croydon around 2pm on Monday. She'd had a late leisurely breakfast with her parents then set off with many promises to keep in touch and let them know 'how things go'.

I reckon they heard me on the phone to Zack yesterday, Allegra thought. They seem to be walking on egg shells this morning, not able to bring themselves to ask me about the call.

Allegra swerved to avoid a rabbit bouncing along merrily, totally oblivious to danger. She fiddled with the radio controls until she found something worth listening to. Ah, heavenly Bach...

As she drove past Stonehenge, Allegra's heart beat faster. She'd visited the site with Zack – a memorable day, with both of them full of love and hope, of plans for the future. Allegra shivered as she recollected Zack holding her hand, marvelling at the huge ancient stones full of history and secrets, remembering how she'd stumbled and he'd caught her before she fell, enfolding her in his strong embrace. She swerved again, this time not because of a rabbit, and decided to pull into the next layby she found, realising she needed a break.

Car safely parked, the tears began to flow and once started, she couldn't seem to stop.

"I still love him," Allegra sobbed. "I don't think I can face seeing him this evening without telling him how I feel, but it would be all wrong to do so."

After a while she blew her nose and checked her face in the mirror. Her car rocked slightly as the traffic whooshed past and she realised she felt able to continue on her journey.

"Mirror, signal, manoeuvre," she chanted as she pulled back onto the road. "Full speed ahead! If I don't get a move on, my violin pupil will be at the flat for their lesson before I am!"

In addition to her freelance orchestral commitments, Allegra had eight violin pupils. They had to be super-flexible to fit in around her schedule, which was never the same from week to week. She particularly enjoyed working with youngsters, passing on what she knew and sharing her passion for music.

Allegra was prone to saying she learnt far more from her pupils than they ever learnt from her; when she had said that to one of her pupils once in his lesson, the ten year old, with a cheeky smile to show her he was joking, instantly replied, "Why does my mum pay you then? Shouldn't you pay me?"

Allegra had laughed uproariously, taking the remark in the spirit it was given.

When Allegra finally reached London, she had to drive round for a good ten minutes looking for a space to park before she could make her way upstairs to the top floor flat of Elgin Court.

There was a note on the kitchen table from Holly:

Out at a recording session at Abbey Road Studios – see you later!

Allegra gave the sitting room a quick once over, hiding various clothes waiting to be ironed, and tidied the enormous pile of books and magazines. She got Boris's violin out and tuned it, ready for the lesson. As the doorbell went, she spotted a couple of abandoned coffee cups and plates, and hastily popped them into the tiny kitchen adjacent to the main room.

Within minutes of her arrival, Allegra's pupil, Cassie, was cheerfully playing 'I do like that doggie in the window', while Cassie's mother listened proudly from the sofa.

"You're really coming on!" Allegra enthused. "Your performance was much more in tune than when you played to me last week. Well done! Remember to hold the bow more like this," she demonstrated, "more gracefully, not like a spear or a stick."

"But it is a stick," Cassie said, her eyebrows knitting together.

"Yes, it is, you're quite right," Allegra said, "but the sound will be even sweeter if you try this...and this...yes!"

"Definitely sounds better," Cassie's mum said. "Mind if I take a picture of your hand, Allegra? I'd like to help Cassie get the proper position at home."

"I was about to make the same suggestion," Allegra replied.

"What's that?" Cassie asked, pointing.

"Oh, something very sweet!" Allegra pulled a tiny teddy bear on a loop of ribbon out of Boris's violin case.

"Why's it in there? In your case?"

"I've borrowed the violin – it belongs to a friend of mine."

A friend with a very soft centre, Allegra thought.

"My violin was taken, stolen, in Spain."

"I'm sorry to hear that," Cassie's mum said.

"But why does he keep a teddy in his case? Your friend?" Cassie persisted.

"I don't know," Allegra said. "I think that maybe he's a very sweet man who still loves teddies."

Cassie looked satisfied with the answer, much to Allegra's relief. There was a limit to the number of 'why' questions she felt up to answering each lesson.

"I'll mention the violin to my husband," Cassie's mum said. "As he's in the police, he might be able to help."

"Thank you," Allegra said. "Very kind. The police in Spain don't seem to have had much luck yet. I'd be interested to know if your husband thinks we should be doing anything else."

"You should hire a private detective!" Cassie suggested, her eyes wide with excitement.

Allegra smiled, continuing, "I've shared pictures and a description of the instrument as extensively as I can, but beyond that, I'm not sure else what I can realistically do."

"Leave it with me. I'll see what my other half says and I'll text you. OK?"

Once Cassie and her mother had gone, Allegra felt yet another pang at the loss of her treasured violin.

Boris had strongly recommended a description and pictures of the violin and bow should be widely circulated, as an instrument reported as stolen would be much more difficult to sell on. Everyone in the orchestra and choir had helped with this, using all the usual social media channels to contact musicians throughout the world, and the story had appeared in the local press in Spain, with a picture of Allegra in full concert dress holding her violin, taken in happier times.

There's nothing more I can do at the moment, Allegra thought.

Realising she didn't have long before she needed to leave for her appointment with Zack, she ran into her bedroom and started riffling through her clothes; very soon the floor was littered with discarded garments.

She smiled to herself as she realised it was quite ridiculous to worry about how she might appear to Zack – as if he would be interested! But rationalising this did not stop the panic threatening to engulf her.

They had arranged to meet because he'd suggested it was time they got together as friends and she'd agreed on the phone it would be good thing, to be friends. But her whole body was screaming out that friendship wasn't what she had in mind. She wanted more. She wanted her Zack, her true love, back where he belonged, at the centre of her life.

Chapter 10

Sorting Out Priorities

Allegra sat waiting for Zack in the pizzeria, fiddling with her necklace. In the end she'd decided to wear a dress he'd often admired, a beautiful greenish blue colour, loosely fitted and flowing.

She saw him the moment he appeared at the doorway, her Zack, the light reflecting on his shiny dark curls.

"Sorry!" he said, "Rehearsal ran late, followed by trouble with the bus. Have you ordered?"

"I didn't know what you wanted," Allegra said.

"Same as I always used to have." Zack grinned. "Thick crust, four seasons with extra cheese."

Allegra smiled. "I thought you might have refined your taste since we last ate here."

"No chance!"

Zack looked across the table, eyes twinkling. "It's good to see you. I've often hoped we could meet like this, as friends. There's no reason why not, is there?"

Allegra wanted to scream at him, yes, because I'm in love with you and can't settle for mere friendship, but was saved from potential embarrassment by the arrival of the waiter.

"So," Holly demanded later, "how did it go?"

"We had a lovely meal," Allegra said, "but he wasn't the same, correction, *we* weren't the same. He was polite and attentive, very charming, with lots of amusing stories and gossip about the music business, but I felt I hardly knew him anymore."

"It's been a long time," Holly said. "He must have had a reason to want to meet up with you again. Didn't he want to talk about what had happened between you?"

"Yes, he did. He brought it up almost straight away, almost as if it was a task he had to get over, a chore imposed on him."

Allegra stirred her cocoa and put her legs up on the sofa. She and Holly were both in their dressing gowns, relaxing in the sitting room, nursing their bedtime drinks.

"He was very matter of fact about it – said break-ups happen, it's commonplace, and he entirely understood my reasons for wanting to end our engagement. He said he knew we weren't suited because of what happened, the way we split up, but he would always be fond of me and I'd have a special place in his heart, as a friend."

"But not special enough to get re-engaged?"

Allegra bit her lip. "Didn't seem to have crossed his mind to re-kindle our romance. More a case of explaining its failure and closing the door on it, in a civilised way. I felt I was a loose end that had to be adjusted, possibly removed, before he could carry on with his life. It was almost as if someone had told him he needed to meet up with me again, just the two of us, and make sure there were no hard feelings."

"Don't look at me," Holly said. "I would never try and interfere – I know from experience how it can backfire." She took a sip of her drink. "I know you can't tell me why you broke up with him and as I've said before, I would never expect you to break his confidence, but it *is* hard to understand why you broke up, not knowing the facts."

Allegra thought back to the moment she'd thrown the engagement ring at Zack, the culmination of a lot of emotion and drama.

"Long story short, he'd told me something about his past," Allegra said. "I didn't think it should have been a secret, and told him so. He was becoming obsessed with it; it was eating away at him. He said he couldn't marry me until he'd found the answer.

"It made me very concerned that he thought we shouldn't get married until he'd sorted this out and I wanted instead to help him, to advise and support him, but he wouldn't hear of it, said it was his situation, his problem, nothing to do with me; all of a sudden I realised we were too young to commit to each other, it was all too rushed, and so I behaved in the most childish and hurtful way, by rejecting him. What I wouldn't give to go back in time..."

Holly sighed. "Doesn't mean you can't fix things

now," she said.

"We're not the same people and what we had is well and truly over, at least as far as he's concerned," Allegra said. "I saw his face when we said goodbye outside the restaurant and it had relief written all over it. There wasn't even a hint of him giving me a hug, let alone a peck on the cheek. He'd come with a mission, to smooth over any possible unpleasantness between us, and then, job done, he could move on. I'm a mistake from his past he came to visit, to check on, and now he's happy."

"You could have got this completely wrong," Holly said. "You do know that? It wouldn't be the first time you've misread a situation where Zack's concerned."

"You mean when I thought he was engaged to Vanessa, when I bumped into them at Gatwick?"

"Yes!"

"A different situation," Allegra declared.

"Nevertheless, you should consider the possibility you've misread the situation again," Holly argued. "When Zack asked you to meet for a meal, he might not have been trying to close a door, but instead attempting to make a fresh start. Did you ask him about the, I don't know what to call it, this mystery you keep alluding to?"

"Yes," Allegra said, "and he said he'd made progress, but the way he said it made me feel it wasn't anything to do with me and he didn't want to share details. I felt excluded – just as I had when we were engaged. He always was a very private person."

"It almost sounds as if he were checking up on you, out of concern, to see if you were all right."

"I think he was. And I let him think I was fine," Allegra said sadly. "If he only knew..."

"Maybe you should have been more open with him? Told him how you felt?" Holly suggested.

"No," Allegra whispered. "I didn't want to make it all about me. He obviously still has a lot to sort out and why should I want to burden him with feelings he doesn't want to hear about?"

"It's incredibly late," Holly said as she tidied away the cups they'd been using. "Things will seem better in the morning. I'm back in the recording studio tomorrow. What have you got on?"

"Nothing until the afternoon, thank goodness," Allegra said as she yawned. "A rehearsal, and concert in the evening."

"I've heard from Boris, confirming our tickets for Wednesday." Holly made her way to the door.

"He's so kind," Allegra said as she switched off the side lights in the sitting room, "and he seems pretty keen on you."

Holly smiled. "I think you'll find it's *you* he's keen on."

Allegra stared in amazement. She was sure Holly and Boris were made for each other.

"Yes, definitely!" Holly said. "You can't see it because of your feelings for Zack. Remember how helpful Boris was in Spain, when your violin was stolen? And lending you his violin – above and beyond the call of duty, surely?"

"He's a lovely guy," Allegra said, "and I'm sure he would've done the same for anyone. It's good to know I've got friends like you, Holly, and Boris, looking out for me. Helps my feelings for Zack to start to evaporate. I'll soon be able to put all this behind me."

Despite her comments, Allegra knew full well her feelings for Zack showed no signs of abating, in fact, having seen him so many times in the last week, her feelings were growing ever more intense, if such a thing were possible.

As she lay in her bed that night, her mind went back to the day they had become engaged.

It had been a perfect summer's day – they'd been out for a picnic in the local park, eating hard-boiled eggs and sandwiches, with a flask of tea, fragrant strawberries and fresh apricots. They'd sprawled out under a willow tree, relaxed and happy in each other's company, no need for words, contented and floating in happiness.

"Will you marry me?" they'd both said together, then pulled towards each other, hugging, kissing, laughing, deciding how to tell everyone, and planning for the future.

That had been the turning point, Allegra thought. It had started to go wrong on the day they'd became engaged.

From that moment, Zack had seemed to become troubled, weighed down by something. He kept talking about what they would do when they were married, about where they were to live, children, jobs and so on, whereas Allegra was contented to enjoy being engaged and didn't want to make lots of important decisions now – she thought they could face things together if and when circumstances changed. She realised it was important to Zack to have firm plans and tried to understand and accommodate for his more controlling approach to life, but she found it hard. She had confided in her mother, but Cathy had said everyone was different and marriage meant give and take – it would all work out.

One day Allegra had tried to explain to Zack she was confident things would work out naturally – they didn't need to make plans all the time, about a family and so on. Zack had shouted and said it wasn't enough, you had to plan, otherwise terrible situations happened – you only had to look at what had happened to him.

Once he started talking, Allegra thought he would never stop. He poured out his story, all his worries, his fears, how he wanted things to be different when he had a family, how important it was to make sure everything was OK.

Zack told her he had been adopted, as a baby. His mother had been a young, unmarried nurse who had made a mistake and trusted a man who didn't prove himself worthy. She'd been abandoned and felt the best option for her unborn child was to put it up for adoption.

"But Zack, I didn't even know you'd been adopted," Allegra had said. "Why did you wait until now to tell me this?"

Zack's face was a picture of misery and Allegra put her arms round him in a trice. "Thank you for telling me," she whispered. "It must have been a hard secret to keep."

Zack said he'd had the happiest of childhoods with his adopted parents. To their great joy, after thinking they couldn't have children and adopting Zack, they'd managed to produce his brother Joe the year after Zack's arrival; the two boys grew up as close as brothers can be, sharing everything except looks. Zack was tall and dark, whereas Joe was shorter, with blond hair and blue eyes. If anyone noticed how different the two brothers were, they didn't comment on it, and the family chose not to talk about the adoption outside their small family circle, almost as if it had never happened, but as if Zack and Joe were natural brothers, which was exactly how they felt. They thought it was for the best.

When Zack fell in love with Allegra he began, almost for the first time, to contemplate his own beginning in life.

"I keep thinking about my natural mother," he'd said to Allegra. "I want to know where she is, find out if she wants to see me, if she ever regretted giving me away..."

Allegra sat up in bed, realising she wasn't going to

be able to get to sleep with these memories swirling round and round. She got up and padded to the kitchen to make some tea. Waiting for the kettle to boil, she relived the next stage of the story – the stage when she and Zack had split up.

"I wasn't understanding enough," she whispered. "I could have been much more mature about it all, but instead, I was thinking about myself. I wanted him to come to terms with his adoption instantly, so we could get married and have our happy ever after...I didn't give poor Zack the support he deserved."

She remembered the fateful day she'd gone round to see Zack, having decided he needed a few home truths instead of wallowing in self-pity. He'd been given to a lovely family – what was his problem? Allegra groaned as she recollected how thoughtless and selfish she'd been, showing such a complete lack of understanding. She'd taken her engagement ring off and waved it under Zack's nose, saying,

"Maybe we shouldn't get married!"

The day before, Allegra had been at her parents' house in Bath and Maeve had dropped by, as she often did. Allegra had unwittingly found herself telling Maeve all about Zack acting oddly, without specifically telling her the reason, because he'd asked her not to share the news, even with her family, about him being adopted. This was another reason she felt he was being unreasonable because it was so difficult not to tell anyone at all! Anyway, Maeve had given Allegra some of her usual advice, coloured by her somewhat jaundiced view of the male of the species, and Allegra found Maeve's words crept into her mouth as she confronted Zack.

"You need to sort out your priorities, Zack!" she had yelled.

Zack had been shocked to hear her harsh words and it had been easy then, really easy, to throw the ring at him and run.

As she'd fled, Allegra remembered too late how desperately proud Zack was of being given the ruby engagement ring by his grandmother to pass onto the woman he chose to be his bride. It meant so much to him, as some might have thought Joe should have it, as a 'proper' blood member of the family, but his grandmother had made a point of saying,

"Zack, you're the elder and you are to have it. You're the first boy in this generation. That's final."

I couldn't have been more unkind if I'd planned it for a year, Allegra thought. She felt so ashamed.

Chapter 11

A Day Out In London

"Sure you'll be all right on your own?" Cathy asked Pete.

She'd got up very early, looking forward to her trip to London.

"Of course – you enjoy your day out with Maeve. I'll have a late supper waiting for when you get back," Pete reassured her.

"I could pick something up on the way home?"

"Are you suggesting I'm not capable of preparing a simple meal?" Pete asked.

Cathy raised an eyebrow.

"Point taken! I'm cooking something much simpler today. I emailed my tutor and explained about the quiche; she suggested I tried to prepare lamb chops and salad."

"Mmm, sounds nice!"

"I have to photograph the finished meal to show the class on Thursday. We get marks for presentation," Pete said.

"So you're going to continue with the course?"

"Yes. I feel much more positive about it now. I was reading something by that popular chef, you know, the lady who won Bake-off, the famous one, and she said a good meal doesn't have to take ages to prepare. She even suggested some ways to cheat, like using tinned potatoes for a potato salad, that sort of thing."

Cathy smiled approvingly. The less Pete used the cooker, the better, in her opinion, especially when she was out. If she was in, she could intervene, as she'd done when he'd cooked the veg last Sunday, but Cathy knew she couldn't relax looking round an art gallery or flitting through the shops in Oxford Street if she thought her home was about to catch fire.

"I know what you're thinking." Pete grinned. "I know you too well, Cathy, after nearly thirty five years of marriage! And I'm insulted. I was going to offer you a lift to the train station but I think you can make your own way now!"

"I'd prefer to walk," Cathy replied. "It's a beautiful day and I've got plenty of time. I arranged to meet Maeve at the ticket barrier at 8 – no need to rush."

"I was kidding," Pete said. "Sure you don't want a lift?"

"Quite sure. Good luck with your homework. See you later."

"Have a lovely day and give Maeve my best!"

Maeve and Cathy chattered away nonstop on the journey.

"And how's Allegra getting on?" Maeve boomed.

"What happened when she met up with Zack?"

"She didn't say much," Cathy replied, keeping her voice as quiet as possible, in an attempt to encourage Maeve to do likewise. Quite a few interested heads had already swivelled in their direction during the journey, eager to hear what Maeve's views were on the state of the pavements, the bin collections and the government. Now the conversation had moved on to family matters, Cathy hoped Maeve would be a little more discreet.

"She said she had an interesting time. They had pizza. Tiramisu for dessert."

"Is that all you have to tell me?" Maeve roared. "I expected something a bit more juicy! Really? No gossip at all?"

Cathy cringed in her seat.

"It's a nice view, isn't it?" she asked. "Out of the window?"

Maeve stared at the railway embankments covered in scrubby grass and spindly wildflowers. There were piles of odd misshapen metal pipes strewn about a disused part of the track; a view of the back walls of neglected terrace houses appeared as they drew ever closer to the big city.

"Not much of a view," she said. "Ah, I get it. Sorry! Bit slow on the uptake today. I know I can be too loud. Apologies."

Maeve had a voice that could cut through glass – it had been very useful in her role as Head of Shelley Primary School, but could be a bit overwhelming at close quarters.

Very soon the two friends were walking through the Turner Galleries in Tate Britain.

"Look!" Maeve said. "The size of that canvas! Must have taken ages to paint."

"Mm, fantastically intense," Cathy murmured. "Sensational use of colour."

"Do you think he was short-sighted?" Maeve asked.

"Short-sighted?"

"The pictures look rather blurry and out of focus – a bit like my vision when I go downstairs to breakfast without remembering to pop my specs on," Maeve continued. "I wondered if Turner got the idea of smudging all the colours and edges together because he was short-sighted."

"I think he was heavily influenced by the French Impressionist painters..." Cathy began.

"Were they short-sighted too? I suppose they didn't have proper opticians in those days. Aren't we lucky to have been born in this century?"

As soon as they decently could, the two made a bee-line for the sleek and stylish café in the basement and started wolfing down pastries and flat whites.

"This croissant is delicious," Cathy remarked. "Fresh as can be."

"Mgwahba gumpbump," Maeve replied. "Oh, excuse me, shouldn't talk with my mouth full, naughty me! I meant yes, completely scrumptious."

Some serious chewing and slurping followed – gastronomic bliss.

"Do you remember that school trip we went on," Maeve said, eyes dancing, "when Allegra was ten years old – when we went to Paris?"

"Do I?" Cathy beamed. "Such fun..."

"Ladies," a voice said. "Sorry to trouble you, but would you mind if I plonked myself here, right at the corner of your table? There doesn't appear to be any room elsewhere and..."

"Of course, welcome!" Maeve said. "I'm Maeve and this is my friend, Cathy. I'll budge up a bit, there – all fine."

"We'll be off in a minute," Cathy said. "Nearly finished."

"Please don't go on my account. I'm Boris, by the way."

As Boris held out his hand to Cathy, Maeve gave a sudden shriek.

"Are you a singer? Tell me you're a singer?"

"Yes, I am, but..."

"I knew it! This is similar to what happened last week in one of my programmes...my goodness, this is fate, with a vengeance! With knobs on!"

"Not quite sure I catch your drift..."

"You're Boris! Boris the bass! The singer!" Maeve's face grew increasingly animated. "You rescued a whole bunch of musicians last week in Barcelona by stepping in to conduct a rehearsal – you saved the day and no mistake."

"Why, thank you," Boris said. "My goodness, I

had no idea the story had been so widely reported in the press."

"I'm Allegra's mother," Cathy said. "We've heard all about you and your incredible kindness in lending her your violin. We're very grateful."

"I've heard of coincidence, but this is astonishing!" Boris said. "Stand by ladies; this calls for another round of pastries. Wait until I tell Allegra. She'll be flabbergasted!"

"We know you're taking her to the opera tomorrow," Maeve said.

"The Barber of Seville," Cathy added.

"My word!" Boris leapt to his feet. "You know my life history!"

Once Boris had joined the queue to buy more treats, Maeve leant forward and said, thankfully in a quieter voice than usual,

"Do you think he's 'the one'? That Allegra will marry?"

Chapter 12

A Night At The Opera

"There he is!" Holly shouted. "Look! Over there!"

Allegra waved frantically to Boris through the throngs of people in Covent Garden foyer, all eagerly anticipating an extraordinary evening's entertainment.

"You both look fabulous!" Boris said, giving both Holly and Allegra an affectionate hug.

"It's so exciting!" Holly squealed. "A real treat. A box at the opera – you are kind to share this with us, Boris."

Boris smiled. "My friend in the chorus managed to get his hands on the tickets for me. He said he'd like to meet up with us afterwards – is that OK? Thought we might all go for a drink, maybe a bite to eat?"

"It would be lovely to meet him," Allegra said. "Neither Holly nor I have to be up particularly early tomorrow – nothing to stop us, is there?"

"One of the best things about being a musician." Holly chuckled. "You scarcely ever have to get up early!"

"Oh, not sure about that." Boris pointed to his

face. "See? The black rings under my eyes? I'm still suffering from having to get up exceedingly early on Monday. I had to be at the station at 6.30am to catch a train to Yorkshire. I was judging the singing competition at my old school."

"Sounds fun!" Holly clapped her hands. "You'll have to tell us all about it, maybe later?"

"Point taken. We need to get to our seats. This way, ladies. And may I say how beautiful you both look this evening?"

"You've scrubbed up pretty well yourself," Holly said.

"Yes, not bad," Allegra added.

Boris put his elbows out to the side and Holly and Allegra linked arms with him, ready to join the chattering crowds making their way up the wide expensively carpeted steps.

"Who did you say will be here tonight?"

"Really?"

"Five *thousand*...for one performance?"

"Surely not..."

"But in the papers it said that's the fee he commands nowadays."

"They'll say anything in the papers...I simply don't believe it..."

"No idea who everyone's talking about," Allegra said, "But it sounds exciting."

"Some sort of celebrity?" Holly asked.

"They're exaggerating," Boris said. "Must be. After all, they're talking about Zack."

"Zack's here?" Allegra pulled her arm away from

Boris.

"Apparently he's been invited to see what he thinks of the production," Boris said. "He's made quite a name for himself recently and taking over at the last minute in Barcelona has enhanced his reputation even more. Rumour has it there might be a job opportunity winging its way from the opera house, sooner rather than later."

"But you're the one who saved the day out in Spain," Holly said, squeezing Boris tightly to her side. "Without you we'd all have been completely under-rehearsed."

"Zack's amazing," Boris said, "though it's kind of you to flatter me, Holly. Now, here we are. Our box. We've got it to ourselves tonight – sit in whichever chair you want."

The three friends pulled chairs right to the front of the box and surveyed the orchestra, picking out faces they knew.

"The double bass player from Dubai!" Holly said. "Looks like he's an extra for the evening."

"And the oboist – she looks very familiar," Allegra said. "I'm sure I've worked with her before."

Boris started waving madly at some friends of his in the stalls below.

"Wahay!" he yelled and gave them a massive thumbs up.

Several heads swung round towards the box in a startled fashion.

"Boris!" Holly said. "Do you have any idea how loud your voice is?"

"Sorry." Boris bowed his head in mock repentance. "I've been asked that before, many times. They're old chums, you see, old school friends. Haven't seen them in a while."

"Boris," Allegra said, "you don't have to apologise for having a voice capable of carrying across a crowded theatre. Isn't that what you spent years having your voice trained for?"

"Good point." Boris threw back his head and opened his mouth, as if to test the power of his lungs again, then collapsed laughing. "Don't worry Holly," he choked, "I won't embarrass you again!"

"Idiot!" she said, swatting him with her programme.

They're getting on like a house on fire, Allegra thought. I think they'd make a great couple. I can't believe Holly thought he was keen on me – it's obvious how much he likes her. Oh dear; I'm starting to sound like an interfering old match maker, a bit like Maeve. Although she's almost a match breaker, as well as match maker.

Allegra felt ashamed for her less than generous thoughts about Maeve and her eyes filled with tears of self-pity as she reminded herself yet again what a terrible mistake she'd made, breaking things off with Zack.

A tingling ran through the audience as the lights dimmed and in no time, the vast crowd was transported to eighteenth century Seville; everyone was enchanted by beautiful melodies, rooting for true love and chortling at the comic turns.

"Glad you're born in this century, Holly?" Boris asked in the interval. "You get to choose who you marry, not have your future planned by your guardian, given away to the highest bidder, like our poor heroine."

"Absolutely!" Holly's eyes sparkled with anger. "The way woman were treated, it's, it's...words fail me."

"It's a story!" Boris reminded her.

"And there's a happy ending coming up," Allegra added, "at least I think there is, if my memory isn't playing tricks."

"Oh yes," Boris said. "Quite a complicated plot, pretty ludicrous..."

"Aren't they all?" Allegra interrupted.

"Quite!" Boris agreed. "Ah, bang on time," he continued as there was a knock at the door. "Here's our refreshment. Ladies? Take a glass, if you please."

"Champagne!" Holly shrieked. "Boris! You are divine. What have we done to be spoiled like this?"

"You've been your wonderful self," Boris murmured, "I mean, yourselves," he added, turning to include Allegra.

"My mother and Maeve are still raving about what a gentleman you are," Allegra said, a playful smile on her lips.

"Of course!" Boris said. "It was an absolute pleasure to see them at the Tate. Who'd have thought it? Such a coincidence!"

"Almost like an opera plot," Holly added. "I haven't spotted Zack, by the way – have either of you?"

"No." Allegra's voice was small and tight.

"No sign of him." Boris frowned. "He was supposed to be here, or at least that's what everyone was saying before."

"What happens next, Boris?" Holly asked. "In the plot, I mean."

"Ah, you're going to love the second half," Boris said, "because it begins with the hero disguised as a singing teacher...pretty close to my heart, this bit...and completely hysterical too, you wait and see."

Act 2 passed in a delightful jumble of comedy, farce, heavenly music and poignant feeling, until at last, inevitably, after all the intrigue and innuendo, the mystery and the muddle, love, glorious true love, flourished as it should.

As the curtain went down for the last time, Allegra realised they'd been mistaken. Zack *was* in the audience, right down in the stalls, at the end of the front row. She hadn't noticed him at first. He was wearing a dinner jacket and had his hair neatly combed back, his curls for once tamed to polished perfection. Next to him was a woman with shoulder length wavy hair – he had her hand clasped in his.

The clapping intensified as the soloists took their curtain calls.

"Thank you Boris," Holly said. "What a great evening!"

"Yes," Allegra echoed. "You're so thoughtful and

kind."

Boris put his arms round Holly and Allegra, hugging them both affectionately. He gave Holly a peck on the cheek.

Allegra fixed her gaze on Zack again and as fate would have it, he turned to look up and their eyes locked across the vast amphitheatre.

Allegra felt her heart beat more loudly than the drums had in the opera performance. How could no one hear? The sound was echoing, echoing round the auditorium. Da dum, da dum, da dum, faster and faster.

"Mustn't leave you out, Allegra," Boris said, the champagne flowing freely in his veins, and he reached over to give her a kiss on the cheek.

Zack scowled as he looked up at the trio; he turned back to his neighbour in the seat beside him and whispered something in her ear.

Not again, Allegra thought, her cheeks flaming scarlet. Zack saw me kiss Boris in the restaurant in Spain, then he noticed Boris hug me on the plane – he didn't seem to be happy about that – and now he's seen Boris kiss me. What must he think? If he minds, which he seems to, does this mean he still has feelings for me? But if he does, why didn't he mention them the other night when we had a meal together?

More to the point, who is his mysterious companion?

Chapter 13

A Chance Meeting

"Thank you Boris, but I've a bit of a headache. You go on with Holly and have a meal together. Thank you so much for a lovely evening."

"If you're sure? I don't like the thought of abandoning you like this," Boris said. "Will you be all right getting home?"

"Of course." Allegra smiled encouragingly at Boris and Holly. She didn't see why they should have to change their plans because she wasn't feeling too well. Her head had started throbbing when Zack had turned to look at her in the opera house and all she wanted to do was go home and lie down – however, it didn't mean the others shouldn't enjoy themselves.

"I should come back with you," Holly offered. "I don't like to think of you travelling by yourself. It isn't right."

"Honestly, it's nothing," Allegra insisted. "I'm over-tired. I've had a great evening but I'm happy to go home now. Besides, you two will enjoy being alone together." She winked at Holly, who blushed furiously.

"Shame my friend the tenor wasn't able to join us," Boris said, "but I can catch up with him another time. He's decided he should have an early night – got to be up at the crack of dawn to catch a plane to France – his agent called him this evening saying there was a sudden opportunity due to some soloist being ill, and would he like to sing in 'The Messiah'. Lucky him! I'd jump at a chance like that."

"Bit like when Zack was able to conduct at short notice, to help out when Rostopovsky was ill," Holly said.

"Indeed!" Boris turned to Allegra and said, "Let us at least walk you to the tube. It's on our way – I insist."

"Thank you," Allegra said.

The three friends made their way through the crowds to the underground station and with many more apologies and lashings of sympathy, Boris and Holly went on their way.

Allegra pulled her jacket around her as she made her way down to the platform, choosing to take the stairs. She wasn't fond of lifts and thought the exercise might help to clear her head. Not that there's much fresh air down here, she realised as she breathed in the thick stale atmosphere.

The platform was thronged with people, many clutching opera programmes and talking excitedly about the thrilling evening they'd had. As Holly boarded the train, she spied an empty seat and made a bee-line for it, only to find an elderly gentleman in greater need hovering nearby.

"Please, have this seat," she said, indicating the vacant space.

"Thank you my dear," he said.

"Allegra! Here – take my seat," a voice said, a voice Allegra hadn't expected to hear this evening, a voice she heard all the time in her head, a voice belonging to the person she was head over heels in love with – Zack.

"Thank you," she whispered and sat down gratefully.

"Not with your friends?" Zack asked.

"Boris and Holly have gone out for a meal but I'm not feeling a hundred per cent, so I'm on my way home."

"Boris should have taken you home."

"I can manage. He doesn't own me you know."

Zack's eyes burned into her. "A gentleman would take his girlfriend home," he insisted.

"He's not my boyfriend," Allegra said. "I don't know why you should think he is – he's actually very fond of Holly, as she is of him. Not that there's anything settled between them; they haven't know each other long, but I think I know Holly well enough..."

"Are you match-making?" Zack asked.

"No!" Allegra smiled. "I really do have a headache, but I also know they don't mind being left together – that's a bonus and stops me feeling guilty because I know I haven't ruined their evening, in fact I've probably made it better for them. Another friend of Boris's was meant to be joining us, but he cried off at the last minute – a work commitment…"

"Had Boris set you up with a blind date?" Zack asked.

Allegra looked at him, surprised. She wondered why he was being a little *possessive*, for want of a better word.

"I don't think it was a blind date," she replied. "I think it would have been four friends out for a meal after a lovely evening at the opera."

Zack stared out of the window, clenching and unclenching his fist.

"I presume you're going to Victoria?" he said.

"Yes. And you?"

"Still in the same flat in Clapham," Zack said. "So, yes."

Should I ask him about the woman he was with, wondered Allegra. It's none of my business, but he's been asking me all sorts of questions.

"Did you enjoy the performance?" she asked.

"Yes."

"I heard you might be working at Covent Garden soon."

"Who told you?" Zack asked.

"I think it was Boris. Some other people were saying things too – members of the audience."

"It's a possibility," Zack said. "We shall see."

"It sounds a very exciting possibility," Allegra enthused. "Congratulations! It's a real feather in your cap."

Zack broke into a smile, making his whole face light up.

"I'd forgotten how enthusiastic you were about everything, and how generous you are with your praise. How's the headache, by the way?"

"Lifting." Allegra stood up. "We need to change here to another tube line."

By the time they reached Victoria, her headache had completely disappeared. They made their way to the gigantic notice board in front of the platforms and looked for the Brighton line, for trains to Clapham and Croydon.

"Oh no," Allegra said in dismay. "There's a long delay. It'll be at least forty minutes."

"It's usually such a good service," Zack said. "I wonder what could be wrong?"

"It'll be nothing. A leaf on the line or something quite trivial." Allegra sighed and tucked her hair behind her ear. "You should go home using a different route, Zack – lots of trains on other lines go through Clapham. Don't let me hold you up."

"I've a better idea," Zack said. "We could go for a walk. It's not far to St James Park."

"It's a long way," Allegra said, "and it's quite late. Will St James be open? Surely the London parks don't stay open at night?"

"There's one way to find out," Zack said, a huge grin taking over his handsome face, the corners of his mouth curling up attractively.

"Tell you what," Allegra suggested, "I reckon we've got time to walk to Buckingham Palace, right on the edge of the park, before we have to turn round and come back for our train. I'm up for it if you are."

"Race you!" Zack shouted.

As she hared along the streets with Zack, Allegra felt happier than she had for a long time. She was glad she hadn't asked him about the woman he'd been with at the opera. Didn't Boris say Zack had been invited to attend the performance because he might be offered some conducting there? The woman was probably part of the management of the opera house. Or she might be his agent. Something similar.

But he was holding her hand at one point, Allegra remembered, feeling uneasy. Although, she reasoned, Boris gave me a kiss but that didn't mean anything except friendship.

Allegra frowned a little as she tried to square the idea of a professional partnership with a job offer looming, with holding someone's hand – and failed miserably.

I'll ask him, she thought. When the time is right. If I feel brave enough.

Very soon the pair arrived in front of the floodlit palace. Allegra gazed up at the monumental building, home to some of the most famous characters in British history over the last couple of hundred years or so.

"It's so romantic!" Allegra clasped her hands together. "I can imagine the young Queen Victoria inside, with her beloved Prince Albert. Such a tragedy he died young."

"You should live in a palace." Zack came closer to her, so close she could breathe in the tangy citrus smell of his aftershave. Old memories flooded her senses and she began to tremble.

Allegra turned to face him, the tension between them unbearable. As he bent his head down, she closed her eyes for a second, then stepped back in alarm, frightened of what might happen next.

Determined to break the mood, she said brightly, "A palace? You think I should live in a palace? Are you suggesting the lovely flat I share with Holly is anything less than a palace?"

Zack looked down at the gravel. "I meant..." he began as Allegra, gathering her courage, continued,

"Do you mind my asking, who was the lady you were with this evening? At the opera?"

"Someone very dear to me," Zack said softly. "Someone I haven't known long, yet I feel as if I've known her forever. I hope she'll always be part of my life."

Allegra was silent as she contemplated the enormity of what Zack was saying. I had no right to ask him, she thought. I have no claim to him. What nearly happened between us just now, the kiss, the kiss that never was, means nothing. I threw my chance of happiness away when I chucked the ring at him. This serves me right. Of course he's met someone else. Why wouldn't he? Talented, good-looking, famous and successful too – no doubt he has women from all the corners of the world pursuing him...

"Sorry – text – got to look at this," Zack said, getting his phone out of his pocket.

Allegra knew instinctively it was from *her* when she saw Zack's perfect face soften and crease into a smile as he read the text.

"I'm glad you're happy," she said stiffly. "My goodness, I think we have to get back – our train will be arriving shortly."

Zack looked up from his phone, one eyebrow raised.

"Ah," he said. "I see what you're thinking, Allegra. The text is from the lady at the opera. She's everything to me because I've been looking for her for so long. It's like a new life – I can hardly explain..."

"Who is she?" Allegra asked, light dawning.

"She's my mother."

Chapter 14

Zack's Past Is Revealed

"His mother? Allegra, what on earth are you talking about?"

Cathy sat down at the kitchen table feeling rather perplexed as she chatted to her daughter on the phone on Thursday morning.

"Is that unusual? For him to have seen his mother? Or to get a text from her?"

"Mum, you don't understand the significance. Let me explain..."

"His mother?" Cathy repeated. "She's such a nice lady. Remember when we all went out for a lovely lunch, shortly before you got engaged? Your father and I clicked straight away with both of Zack's parents...and of course I got to know his mother pretty well when we worked together to arrange your engagement party..."

"Mum!" Allegra interrupted in an exasperated tone.

"Yes?"

"Please listen. There's something you don't know. I couldn't tell you before, because Zack didn't want me to, but he doesn't mind people knowing now."

"Ah," Cathy said. "I thought there was something. His mother once said to me in an unguarded moment she was sure Zack would share his news with us at some point but they'd always taken the line he should be the person to say. I wondered at the time what she meant. So, what is the big secret?"

Cathy frowned as all sorts of explanations thronged into her mind – no, she wouldn't go there.

But if Maeve had been listening, Cathy mused, she would have come up with all sorts of possibilities – a secret first disastrous marriage like Mr Rochester in 'Jane Eyre', maybe a spell in the Young Offenders' Institute after an unfortunate mistake in his youth...but that would be Maeve, Cathy thought as she put these unbelievable ideas behind her and closed the door on them very firmly.

Maeve found it hard to separate normal life from fantasy – Cathy wasn't going to make the same mistake.

"The big secret is, Mum, Zack was adopted as a baby."

"Is that all? Sorry – I didn't mean to make light of the situation – of course, it must be a big thing to deal with...Is Joe adopted? No, I see...explains why the two brothers look utterly different. It had never occurred to me to wonder why before...and you say Joe's engaged now?"

"Yes, to Vanessa," Allegra said.

"Vanessa – what a lovely name...anyway, carry on with telling me about Zack. Your father and I had no idea he'd been adopted."

"He didn't tell me until after we became engaged," Allegra said. "He found it very difficult to talk about and I think it made him anxious for the future, about having a family of his own."

"Oh Allegra," Cathy said, "I wish you'd been able to tell me all this. Such a thing for Zack to face, and for you."

"He didn't want me to say anything at the time," Allegra said, "so I couldn't."

"You've always been very loyal and good at keeping confidences," Cathy remarked, "but I can see how challenging it must have been, and I'm pleased he doesn't mind you talking about it now."

"I knew you'd understand, Mum."

"Allegra," Cathy began, "was this why, I mean, tell me to mind my own business, but was this anything to do with why you and Zack split up?"

There was a long silence from the other end of the phone.

"Sorry darling," Cathy said. "I shouldn't have asked."

"It had something to do with it," Allegra said, "but we split up mostly because I wasn't able to offer Zack the support he needed..."

Cathy spent some time talking to Allegra, reassuring her and trying to comfort her.

"In the end," Cathy said to Pete once the call was ended, "I told her how much we loved her and said

I thought she'd done the best she could at the time. We none of us find it easy to cope with the big issues in life and it sounds as if she and Zack were overwhelmed with the enormity of his situation."

"None of it sounds a walk in the park," Pete agreed. "But I have to say, if they couldn't cope, perhaps they weren't meant to be together."

"I disagree," Cathy said softly. "I think they are perfect for each other and it's one of the things I feel saddest about. Allegra met the love of her life and it was all going swimmingly; somehow she managed to let him slip through her fingers, or perhaps circumstances conspired against them."

"You could be right, but we shouldn't interfere," Pete reminded Cathy.

"I know but it's tempting," she said. "What I wouldn't give to put the two of them in the same room together and force them to talk to each other honestly. I'm sure they'd be able to sort things out."

"But it's been a whole year since they split up," Pete said. "A lot of water under the bridge."

"I'm never completely sure what people mean by 'water under the bridge', but you're probably right." Cathy sighed. "They're not the same people they were. I know Allegra's changed since they split up."

"And we don't even know about Zack," Pete continued, "not having seen him for a long time. He's a big name in the classical music world. Does Allegra even know if he's attached? A man like that, with the world at his feet..."

"Allegra says he's not with anyone else," Cathy said.

Pete scratched his head. "And what about the meal on Monday? Why did Zack want to meet up with Allegra?"

"Apparently it was Zack's mother's idea, his birth mother. Allegra said he'd told her all about being engaged and how it had ended abruptly. She thought he should meet up again properly with Allegra, after meeting her unexpectedly on tour which had been awkward for both of them, initially at least. She said he should have a good chat with Allegra and make sure they could be friends, particularly as they were bound to work together again in the future, now his career's taken off."

"Sounds sensible," Pete said. "It can't have been easy for either of them to suddenly see each other in Barcelona after splitting up last year; if they're friends they won't have to dread running across each other again, will they?"

"It may *sound* sensible," Cathy said, "but I'm not sure it's true, not if, as I suspect, Allegra's still in love with Zack. Oh, why are affairs of the heart always complicated?"

"Love will find its way through paths where wolves fear to prey," Pete remarked.

"What? Pete!" Cathy could scarcely believe her husband was quoting romantic poetry. He was still able to surprise her.

"Lord Byron." Pete cleared his throat. "He knew

a thing or two about love. One of my favourite quotes; tended to trot it out in the A' level English lessons when I was teaching."

"I see. And the relevance? Despite being a desperately romantic saying, I'm not sure it applies in this situation. What do wolves have to do with it?"

"I mean," Pete said, "that we don't need to worry unduly. If Zack and Allegra are meant to be friends, well, they are friends again now – no problem. If there's meant to be more ahead for them, then 'Love will find its way', even if the path is difficult, a path fierce creatures like wolves would be scared to take."

"You think our job is to stand back and let love get on with it?" Cathy asked.

Pete put his arms round Cathy. "Yes. You certainly don't need to worry about it – not as much as you do, anyway."

"But worrying is part of my job description," Cathy said.

Pete planted a tender kiss on his wife's cheek and picked up the apron from the hook on the back of the kitchen door.

"I need to make haste," he said. "I'll see you anon, after my cookery lesson. Let's hope the tutor sets an easier homework this week."

"Indeed." An image of the burnt quiche flashed into Cathy's mind.

"Know what you're thinking," Pete said with a chuckle. "What have you got planned for the day? Is it the charity shop, or one of your reading ladies?

I can't keep up with all your good works."

"Volunteer library delivery for Mrs Oatcake – she's got through the books I took round last week very quickly and is desperate for more – then yoga class, to cope with the stress of my life. After that, I'm having coffee with Maeve before we do a charity shop shift together."

"Ah ha!" Pete beamed with pleasure. "Gives me a chance to tell you one of my special yoga jokes. I've been saving this one up..."

Cathy groaned. "No! Please!"

"When you get to your yoga class, enjoy the 'Worrier Pose'." Pete sniggered. "Get it? Worrier? Not 'Warrior Pose', but Worrier...? Your favourite pose."

"I got it." Cathy sniffed. "Just didn't think it was funny."

"No offence meant my darling. Besides, I know you're not really offended because I can see you're trying hard not to smile, but failing miserably."

Cathy's shoulders started to shake with the effort of not laughing.

"See you later. Don't bother about supper because I'll bring something back from cookery class; we're making hotpot today."

The phone rang as soon as the front door had clicked shut.

"Hello? Mum – I've got some exciting news!"

"Allegra! Is it Zack? Are you and he...?"

"No. Nothing like that. It's to do with one of my pupils, Cassie – her father is a policeman, high up in the Met. He's taken an interest in my missing violin and rang me a few minutes ago to say that – at long last – it's been found!"

Chapter 15

Allegra's Violin

Allegra hurried to the police station to collect her violin, almost tripping over her own feet in her anxiety to be reunited with the instrument.

"Thank you! I'm enormously grateful...oh, how disappointing, I'm afraid this isn't mine."

Allegra looked at the cheap case the policeman had in front of him on the table and struggled to hold back the tears.

"Now you wait a minute, before you decide," the policeman said. "Take a good look inside the case..."

"Oh, how wonderful! Yes officer, thank you. This is my violin, but in a different case."

"It's very common for a thief to change the case," the policeman advised. "Some cases have tracker devices in."

"Oh, I didn't have anything like that!"

The policeman smiled. "The violin looks un-harmed. Those scratches and marks are all old, aren't they?"

"Oh, yes officer. The result of being played for, let's see, the violin was made in the late 1880s –

probably over a hundred and thirty years."

Allegra cradled her violin protectively; she'd missed it as much as if it were a person. She reached into the case, murmuring,

"Still got my lovely bow, too. Glad the thief kept it with the violin. The instrument isn't complete without it."

"We think the criminal definitely knew what he or she was doing," the policeman said. "You were probably targeted as you left the rehearsal. They were after a valuable violin and bow, the sort used by a top professional."

"What do you think happened to the case?" Allegra asked. "It wasn't anything special – but if it turns up, I'd be pleased to have it back."

"Of course," the policeman said, "although I have to say it's unlikely it will reappear. It was probably discarded, or sold on immediately after the instrument was stolen."

"I understand, officer. I'm really grateful to have the violin and bow back – the case and other contents are replaceable."

Except for my favourite snaps, Allegra thought sadly, the ones of Zack and me at the seaside, taken in the photo booth. The ones where we're happy and in love, before life got complicated.

After repeating her thanks many times, Allegra set off to East Croydon Station to catch the train up to London, as she had an orchestral rehearsal that afternoon at the Albert Hall followed by a concert in the evening. She was carrying two violin cases – one contained her own dear violin, from which she had already vowed she would never, ever, allow herself to be parted from again on tour, even if it meant holding it on her lap next time she ate in a restaurant, and the other was Boris's.

Allegra managed to leap onto the train as the doors were closing.

"Holly! Great. I was hoping we'd be catching the same train."

"You got your violin back!" Holly said. "Oh, Allegra, I'm really happy for you. Did they tell you more about how it had been found?"

"It was because of something Boris said, you know, about posting on various musical sites about the violin having been stolen, with photos."

"He knows so much about music and everything, doesn't he?" Holly said. "He is an amazing sort of guy."

Allegra smiled. "You're completely smitten, aren't you? I think he feels the same."

Holly blushed. "How can you be sure?"

"It's obvious," Allegra said. "I noticed how very attentive he was towards you at the opera. And when you came home yesterday after your meal, you couldn't stop talking about him."

"I was amazed you were still up when I got home – I thought you would've gone straight to bed with your headache."

"Oh, it got much better. My train was delayed for quite a long time."

"Why do I get the feeling, just like last night, that there's something you're not telling me?" Holly demanded.

"No idea," Allegra said. "You're very imaginative?"

Holly folded her arms. "Intuitive, not imaginative."

"Oh, all right," Allegra said. "There is something, but you'll have to wait. I'm too excited about my violin. Didn't you say you wanted to know how it was found?"

"Yes," Holly said eagerly. "You said it was because of Boris?"

"Because of his excellent advice, the auction houses were on the alert for a stolen violin and sure enough, my violin was offered to a famous auction house in Paris, you know the one, very high prices, the one that's always in the news. Anyway, the police were tipped off, and a man was arrested when he came to deliver the violin and bow to the auction room, mistakenly thinking he was about to get away with selling a stolen instrument. After his arrest, he was eager to spill the beans about how he got the instrument and the police soon managed to trace the chain back to the original thief, who pleaded guilty straight away."

"Wow!" Holly gasped. "Your violin has travelled about a bit since leaving the restaurant."

"Yes," Allegra said, "but luckily it's been carefully looked after."

"They'd have been stupid not to keep it safe, considering its value," Holly remarked.

"Yes, indeed." Allegra patted the case on her lap. "I need to get it checked over to make sure, but it looks fine to me. I can't wait to start playing it again."

She looked at the other violin case she had brought with her, wedged between her knees and resting on her feet. "I had to bring Boris's violin with me because I couldn't be sure my own violin would be in a fit state to play. I'll try to get it back to him as soon as possible; he must have missed playing it."

Holly's face assumed a slightly soppy expression on hearing Boris's name mentioned.

"On the other hand," Allegra said, "maybe he has found a new interest?"

Holly leaned forward. "I haven't forgotten," she said.

"Forgotten what?"

"You think my brain's turned to mush because I'm love struck, but I'm waiting; you promised to tell me what happened after we left you at Covent Garden Tube."

"Oh, that." Allegra peered out of the window. "Look! Nearly at Victoria. Time to get off."

"I insist!" Holly said. "You promised."

"It's nothing," Allegra said. "I happened to meet Zack on the tube. We travelled to Victoria and went for a walk, right up to Buckingham Palace, as the trains were all delayed."

"You went for a late night walk with Zack? What

happened?"

"Thank goodness the trains run all night back to Croydon – we're lucky to live where we do," Allegra said.

"You're doing it again," Holly insisted.

"Doing what?"

"Talking about something else in order to avoid talking about Zack. Come on – what's the news?"

"We need to get out," Allegra said. "Come on."

As the two friends scurried along to the underground, with three violins between them, plus bags containing their concert clothes, Allegra turned to Holly and said,

"He won't mind, if I tell you about his secret – you remember I said there was something I couldn't tell you about him, because it would be breaking a confidence?"

Oh yes," Holly said. "It sounded so mysterious."

"It's not a mystery or a secret now," Allegra said. "It's all out in the open. I was talking to my mum about it this morning on the phone."

They had reached the barriers to get onto the tube line and both fell silent as they negotiated their way with their instruments and bags through the narrow opening, tapping their oyster cards.

"I'll fill you in later," Allegra said. "It'll take time to tell you his story and it'll be best if it's somewhere private. But you should know Zack's much happier. Everything's going to be fine for him now. But there's no hope."

"No hope?" Holly echoed. "What do you mean?"

"No hope of us getting back together," Allegra said. "No hope at all."

Chapter 16

At The Royal Albert Hall

Every time she saw the Albert Hall Allegra felt her spirits lift and today was no exception. The massive bulbous, casserole-like shape stood proudly at the top of the flights of shallow stone steps, welcoming Holly and Allegra as they joined a throng of orchestral players all making their way from Prince Consort Road up to the mighty building. Walking round the giant structure to the Artists' Entrance, Allegra thought of all the times she'd performed there before, starting with when she was a teenager in the National Youth Orchestra.

"Do you remember when we first met?" she asked Holly.

"Certainly do. It was my first orchestral course with the Youth Orchestra and I didn't know a soul. You were so friendly – made me feel at home right away."

Allegra smiled. "You were the same. Both of us newbies together, at the back of the second violins."

"It can be scary going away from home for the first time."

"Don't I know it," Allegra said. "And that archaic school where we stayed and rehearsed – it was like something out of Harry Potter."

"I think Harry Potter might actually have been filmed there if I'm not mistaken."

"Yes, think you're right! But the highlight of the course was performing here, at the Albert Hall," Allegra said.

"Absolutely!" Holly replied. "And here we are again."

The two friends hurried in through the entrance and made their way downstairs to the backstage area. In no time at all, they were seated on the vast wide stage, waiting for the conductor to arrive.

"I'm meeting Boris between the rehearsal and the concert," Holly whispered to Allegra. "He's on his way to an audition but has suggested we meet in Hyde Park for half an hour or so. Do you want to join us?"

"Love to," Allegra said, "as long as I won't be in the way. I don't want to be a gooseberry."

"Don't be silly. Boris always likes to see you."

"I'll give him back his violin," Allegra said. "Seems a good opportunity. He's been so kind, letting me borrow it all this time."

"He is exceptionally kind," Holly said. "He's quite the most..."

"Shh," said the leader of the orchestra. "Conductor's on his way. Let's tune, ladies and gentlemen, shall we?"

The oboist played her 'A' and, section by section,

the musicians carefully tuned their instruments. A percussion player decided to join in the fun by pretending to tune the triangle, much to everyone's amusement.

In the break, Holly and Allegra made their way to Hyde Park, the statue of Prince Albert regarding them from his Memorial as they crossed the busy road.

"Looks fabulous, doesn't he," Allegra said, "after his restoration and refurbishment? Look at the gilt."

Holly screeched with laughter. "I thought you were talking about Boris to begin with," she explained. "He's there, see? Waiting for us. He certainly looks fabulous, but I'm not sure he's been restored or refurbished."

"Or has anything to be guilty about," Allegra added.

"What are you two laughing at?" Boris asked as he greeted them warmly. "And what's this? My violin? Don't tell me – yes? They've found yours at last – I'm thrilled! Hope they've caught the thief."

"It seems half the police in Europe have been involved in tracking Allegra's instrument," Holly said. "Interpol have been busy..."

"Yes, they've caught the thief," Allegra said, "and quite a few of the middle men. Thank you, Boris – I don't know what I've have done out in Spain if it hadn't been for your generosity,"

"Oh, someone would have come up with a violin

for you to borrow, no doubt," Boris said.

"But it wouldn't have been as good as yours," Allegra replied. "I'm very grateful. Thank you."

"My pleasure," Boris said. "I'll do anything for one of Holly's friends."

And with that he linked his arm through Holly's and the three of them set off across the grass, marvelling at the warmth of the September day and how the summer was lingering longer than usual. There were a few crunchy leaves beginning to fall onto the green carpet of grass, but generally speaking, it was as if summer was still in full swing.

"I saw another article about Zack in the paper," Boris said, "all about what a great guy he was for saving the day in Spain and how he has a glittering career ahead of him. Some talk of him going out to Sydney. Been offered some conducting dates over there in Oz."

"A great career opportunity," Holly said.

"And how are things working out for you, Boris?" Allegra asked. "Anything exciting in the pipeline?"

"Yes, as a matter of fact there is," Boris replied. "You remember I went up to my old school, to judge the singing competition? Turns out one of the kid's parents is none other than a big noise in the Musical Theatre world. He heard me give a quick demonstration in the competition when I was adjudicating, and on the strength of that, he's asked me to audition for the main part in a big show he's putting on next year."

"Phenomenal!" Holly squeezed Boris's arm.

"I'm off to meet up with him now," Boris said, "which means, I'm afraid, it's time to leave you two ladies. I'll ring you soon, Holly. 'Bye Allegra."

Boris strode off in the direction of the nearest bus stop, his violin bouncing along as he carried it on his back.

Allegra and Holly continued their walk in companionable silence until Holly ventured, "You look a little fed up."

"Sorry! Trying not to inflict my mood on you," Allegra answered.

"You inflict your mood on me as much as you want," Holly said, "if you think it will do any good – but it's not the answer, is it? Why don't you tell me what happened? We've still got a bit of time before we have to be back. Here, let's sit down on the bench. Enjoy the sun while we can."

"All right. But I don't know where to begin."

"What was the last thing Zack said to you," Holly suggested. "We can start there."

"He said he was seriously thinking of accepting."

"Mysterious!" Holly smiled. "Now you'd better tell me the back story. I can't help if I don't know the facts and you said he didn't mind if you talked about it, because it isn't a secret anymore."

"OK." Allegra settled on the bench and told Holly all about Zack's adoption and how he'd decided once they were engaged that he wanted to find out who his birth parents were, or at least trace his mother.

"He'd always been happy in his adoptive family and that made it difficult at first because he didn't know how his adoptive parents would react if he wanted to find his mother, although they'd constantly reassured him they would be there to support him come what may. They had always thought the day would come when he wanted to know – needed to know – exactly where he came from, and would want to meet his mother."

"How tricky for them all and how sensible his parents sound," Holly said. "Go on. What happened next?"

"I'm not exactly sure," Allegra said. "His need to find his mother created a lot of tension between us; my lack of understanding and immaturity made it all much worse and we split up. My fault."

"Doesn't sound as if it was anyone's fault," Holly said. "It was a particularly difficult and stressful time; you were both faced with a situation you couldn't control or cope with."

"Thank you for not blaming me," Allegra whispered.

"You're blamed yourself enough," Holly said. "Let's think forwards now, not backwards. What can be done?"

"Oh, nothing, nothing at all. Zack's made that abundantly clear. Now he's found his mother, he wants to spend as much time as possible with her."

"But it doesn't mean he can't rekindle his romance with you." Holly frowned.

"Oh, yes it does, I'm afraid." Allegra bit her lip.

"You see, he wants so much to be a part of her life, that he's willing to change his."

"Change his life? In what way?"

"He's thinking of giving up all the regular work he has in Europe and moving to live near his mother, maybe even *with* his mother, in the States, in Washington. She's married to an American and has a family out there. He's got a half-brother and two half-sisters he's never met and he wants to be with them – they're all he thinks about."

"But his future," Holly began, "for example, what about the chance to conduct at Covent Garden? Surely he wouldn't throw a career opportunity away? And Boris mentioned something about Australia."

"He doesn't care about fame and fortune, he said. There's a job going at the American University in Washington, a sudden vacancy due to illness – he's already been interviewed by Skype and they offered it to him straight away. It's for one term initially, but can be extended to a permanent post if both sides are happy by Christmas. It's not his usual thing, more of an academic post with some conducting; it would be a big change. He needs to decide very soon if he's going to accept it."

Allegra lifted her hand to her mouth, pulling it away sharply as she realised she was about to bite one of her nails. She hadn't done that since she was eight years old. She needed to pull herself together.

"And what about you?" Holly asked. "Doesn't he care about you?"

"There's no room for me in his life," Allegra said.

"Did he say that? In those exact words?" Holly asked.

"No, not exactly." Allegra was thoughtful. "He said we'd had something special, but it hadn't stood the test of time; the first difficulty that had popped up, we'd crumbled. He didn't blame me, he blames himself, for being secretive and not allowing me to support him through the situation. But nevertheless, I don't think he sees a future for us."

"He's making the same mistake again," Holly said. "He's not asking you to wait and he's pushing you away instead of letting you help."

"I think the truth is, he doesn't feel about me the way he used to," Allegra said. "He said he hoped I'd meet someone better suited than he'd been. He even said he was surprised I hadn't already met someone else by now – he thought I must have lots of men interested in me."

"Did you make it clear how you felt?" Holly asked. "Did you tell him he was the man for you?"

"No. I couldn't. It wouldn't have been fair to burden him with my feelings."

"So he has no idea how you feel and when you said at the beginning he was seriously thinking of accepting, you mean he might be about to put a hold on his career to go and live in Washington with his mother and her family, with no immediate plans to return to this country. Does that about sum it up?" Holly put her hand up to the sky. "And to top it all off, I think I felt a drop of rain. As if things couldn't get any worse!"

"That's about it," Allegra replied. "The new term at the American University starts early next week – if he accepts the job, I have to forget him."

The heavens opened at this point with one of those sudden autumn storms. As the two friends ran back to the Royal Albert Hall, passing Queen Victoria's beloved husband again on his high plinth, Holly shouted to Allegra,

"Don't give up, Allegra – please don't give up!"

Chapter 17

Cathy Keeps Busy

"Sciatica? Oh Maeve, poor you. I'll be round as soon as I can. 'Bye."

Cathy put her phone down and scribbled yet another task on her list of the day.

Maeve – needs help with the hoovering.

"Hey, let me see." Pete looked over Cathy's shoulder.

Go to library, collect more books for Mrs Oatcake and deliver to her.

"How can one woman read so many books?" he questioned.

"She doesn't read all the ones I pick," Cathy explained. "I'm not too good at picking books, to be honest; I always seem to get it wrong."

"Mm." Pete grunted. "I expect it's a clever ruse to get you back sooner rather than later. Mrs Oatcake wants the company."

"Maybe." Cathy's hand trembled as she held the list. "But I'm still being useful, even if that is the reason."

"You're over-tired," Pete said. "Have you had breakfast yet?"

"Haven't had time," Cathy mumbled. "Been up for ages…"

"I'm making some toast now." Pete grabbed the loaf from the breadbin and started hacking into it. "Toast and marmite. Doctor's orders."

"I always enjoy your toast," Cathy said. "And the hotpot you brought back yesterday from class was delicious."

"Glad you liked it."

"I'm looking forward to the meal tonight. What are you cooking? What was homework this week?"

Pete curled his lip. "The tutor said maybe to try something like macaroni cheese, something simple; I wasn't the only person in the class who'd had a disaster with the quiche last week and she said maybe she'd been a bit over-enthusiastic, expecting us to cook something quite advanced, so this week we're all making a pasta dish. She recommended macaroni cheese for me, but some of the others are allowed to make lasagne."

"Lasagne's quite complicated," Cathy said. "Maybe not impossible," she added hastily after looking at Pete's downcast expression, "but certainly time consuming. You don't want to spend all day in the kitchen, do you?"

"Maybe not. But I don't like being fobbed off with macaroni cheese either. I might try lasagne…"

"Have another look at my list," Cathy said, hoping to distract him.

"Ah yes. Next item."

Shift at the charity shop to cover Maeve as she's

indisposed.

"You do too many shifts," Pete counselled. "I've mentioned this before but you haven't taken a blind bit of notice. And what's this?"

Collect autumn plants from garden centre.

"Garden's looking a bit scruffy," Cathy said. "Could do with some autumn colour."

"We could do that together, at the weekend?" Pete suggested.

"OK," Cathy said, crossing it off the list.

Ironing.

"There's not much ironing, is there?" Pete asked.

"There's a mountain to tackle," Cathy replied. "It's almost filling the spare room now."

"Does it matter?"

"Yes, because Allegra will be staying for a few days next week – she's got a concert coming up in Bristol and she's bringing Holly with her. I need to get both the rooms ready for their visit."

"I'll do the ironing," Pete said, "after I get back from cooking. You know how I like to iron while I watch a film on my tablet."

Cathy nodded gratefully. She was finding life overwhelming. Having looked forward to her retirement for years, she was finding she didn't seem to have as much time to herself as she'd thought she would, but instead, an endless procession of chores and duties seemed to appear each morning as she tried to decide how to spend her day.

Mrs Oatcake was all smiles when Cathy arrived at

her door.

"Come in, come in," she said. "Coffee's made and there's shortbread."

Cathy politely took one of the biscuits and perched on the edge of the sofa in Mrs Oatcake's front room.

"I've been looking forward to your visit all morning," Mrs Oatcake declared. "Now, shall we discuss books?"

"I hope you had fun with the historical novels I chose for you last time," Cathy began a little timidly. "I was worried though, that perhaps the one about Henry the Eighth and his second wife might have been a little too blood thirsty? King Henry did seem to go in for beheadings and torture with monotonous regularity."

"They were all right." Mrs Oatcake curled her lip. "Not very adventurous, though. Not even the Tudor one. Not much violence. You have to remember my favourite television programme is 'Game of Thrones'."

Cathy's eyes took on a dazed look, like a rabbit caught in the headlights.

"To be honest," Mrs Oatcake continued, "I felt you were still palming me off with some tame stories – hope you weren't judging me, thinking at my age I couldn't take the strong stuff?"

"Of course not," Cathy said in shocked tones. "I would never patronise you."

She pulled a couple of books out of her bag to show Mrs Oatcake.

"I wondered about these," she said, offering two books the librarian had recommended Cathy take for Mrs Oatcake.

"They're rather different from my previous choices," Cathy said. "I asked the librarian to help and she said that all the other ladies who have the volunteer home visits seem to love them – but in fact now I look at them properly, I'm not sure they're at all suitable..."

"Ah ha!" Mrs Oatcake almost snatched the books from Cathy's hands in her haste to scan the covers. "Worthless books! Exactly what I've been hoping you'd bring me."

"Worthless books? Oh, I'm sorry." Cathy felt flustered and embarrassed. How could she have got it so wrong again? And yet Mrs Oatcake's face was alight with happiness. What had she meant by 'worthless'?

"Worthless books," Mrs Oatcake repeated. "We were never allowed to read these at school, well, not often. Mostly, we weren't allowed to finish them."

"And you want to read them now?" Cathy's eyebrows had shot up so high, they'd nearly disappeared into her fluffy thick hair.

"Of course! It'll be one in the eye for the nuns. Not that they'd mind at all. It was all pretence, a sort of double bluff."

"I think you'd better give me a bit more information," Cathy said. "I'm feeling a mite confused."

"I'll get some more coffee," Mrs Oatcake said,

"because this might take some time. Back in a minute."

Cathy looked round the sitting room while Mrs Oatcake was in the kitchen, wrestling with her new-fangled coffee machine. She admired the family photos in their silver frames, the ornaments brought back from all corners of the globe and the impressive chess set that had belonged to Mrs Oatcake's dear departed husband.

"Drat!" Cathy could hear from the kitchen, followed by "Double drat!"

She knew from experience not to rush to help Mrs Oatcake; the coffee machine was Mrs Oatcake's pride and joy, bought for her by her son for her birthday, and if she was left alone with it, she would eventually remember how to tame the mighty beast into submission and would return to the front room bearing two deliciously strong coffees – coffees that would be the envy of many of the fancy bars in town.

Whoever thinks older ladies prefer weak tea is very much mistake, Cathy thought with a chortle.

"Here we are, dear." Mrs Oatcake appeared at the door with a precariously balanced tray, staggered to the table and set it down with a bump. "Hot and strong – like my men."

Cathy looked a little shocked to hear this, but Mrs Oatcake waved her hand graciously, as if to bat away any possible offence.

"Something we used to say at school, my dear," she explained. "Completely meaningless but we thought we were very grown up saying it and it had the advantage of annoying the nuns too, our main aim in life of course. Now, where were we? Ah yes. School. You know I went to a convent boarding school? In the 1940s?"

"No, I didn't." Cathy settled back in her seat. She had time, as Pete had crossed off the garden centre visit from her list and he was going to do the ironing too; how lucky she was to have a husband like Pete.

"Well I did." Mrs Oatcake looked into the distance.

"I'm sorry," Cathy said. "How terrible to be parted from your family."

Mrs Oatcake cackled. "We had a whale of a time. Of course we missed our parents but there was a war on and so many children were away from their families that we never felt sorry for ourselves. We spent the whole time haring around the school, larking about. Didn't learn much – not from the lessons, such as they were – but it didn't seem to matter. Anyway, we had a good school library, well, reasonable by the standards of the time. I'm sure the nearby boys' school had a much better one, but that's another story. At the weekend, we were allowed to read what the nuns called 'worthless books'. They were the recently published, contemporary, thrilling books, full of murder and romance. Terribly tame, I'm sure, if you compared them with modern books, but we loved them. Once the weekend was over, we had to return them, whether we'd finished them or not; during the week we were only allowed to read the so-called 'improving' books, mostly the classics and biographies of the Saints. Quite a dull collection if truth be told!"

Cathy's eyes were out on stalks. She'd never heard anything like this before. At least when Pete had confiscated books at school, he returned them at the end of the day.

"It must have been frustrating," Cathy commiserated, "to be halfway through a book, especially an exciting, plot-driven book, and not to be allowed to continue with it until the next weekend."

"It was. We all learnt to speed read, but even so, you invariably tended to be halfway through a really cracking read when you were forced to return it. And there was always the chance it wouldn't be available the next weekend," Mrs Oatcake continued. "We suspected the nuns were reading them themselves, and why shouldn't they? But we never had any definite proof. There was a time when my friend Trixie decide to go and snoop in the nuns' quarters to see if she could find a particular book she was wild for...but I digress.

"It came to be part of our vocabulary that any up-to-the-minute books, books we actually wanted to read, were referred to as 'worthless.' The worthless books I'm hoping to read now are the recently published books, the ones everybody's reading, the exciting up-to-the-minute ones. I don't want you to censor what I read because I'm advanced in years.

I still feel the same inside, the same as I've always done. Besides, my friend Trixie's coming to stay soon and she reads very widely. I'd like to have the chance to discuss worthless books with her."

"I see. And you think these books I've brought today are OK?"

"Absolutely!"

"I was beginning to wonder," Cathy said, "and please don't take this the wrong way, but it was something my husband suggested, and he's often wrong, I hasten to say..."

Mrs Oatcake roared with laughter. "You're about to say you thought I was being a little over-fussy about the books I wanted because I was lonely? How hilarious! That's a very common misconception I believe, among the volunteer library helpers, or so my friends all say. No, I was hoping you'd start bringing me some up-to-date reads, with guts, telling it how it is. I want to read about modern life, warts and all."

"Sorry I got it wrong."

"It's my fault – I should have been more specific. I apologise. I suppose I didn't want you to think badly of me, to know I wasn't interested in those pesky biographies and worthy tomes you've been dragging here. I knew we'd get there in the end."

Cathy grinned at Mrs Oatcake and thought what a marvellously spirited lady she was.

"Tell you what, when you've finished with these two beauties," Cathy said, tapping the bright shiny covers of the recently released wildly successful blockbusters in front of her on the table, "I'll have a go at reading them myself!"

Chapter 18

A Special Delivery
October

"My mum says she's hardly ever in the kitchen these days," Allegra said to Holly as the two were chopping salad in the tiny galley kitchen in their flat.

Holly put her head on one side. "I thought your dad was, how can I put it, *struggling* a little with the culinary arts?"

"You mean he's a useless cook?"

"Yes!"

"He was, but Mum says he's getting really good now. Taking it all very seriously, of course – keeps suggesting they need to buy all sorts of gadgets."

"Gadgets?" Holly pursued her mouth.

"Yes – pasta maker, juicer, that sort of thing."

"Ah yes," Holly said. "To be used once, then stored, junking up the kitchen cupboards."

"Exactly," Allegra said.

"Still, look on the bright side. At least you know what to give him for Christmas."

"Holly! How could you?"

"What?"

"Mention *Christmas.* It's the first of October."

"I've seen Christmas cards for sale." Holly sliced the shrink-wrapped end off a cucumber.

"Shocking!"

"And I heard one of your pupils playing 'Jingle Bells' yesterday," Holly said accusingly.

"Fair cop." Allegra grabbed a spring onion and peeled back the thin outer layer. "And I'm flattered, by the way."

"Flattered? In what way...oh, I get it." Holly's eyes twinkled. "You mean you're flattered because I recognised the tune!"

"Yes! Cassie is getting much better at the violin now," Allegra said.

"Her dad was kind, wasn't he," Holly said, "to take a personal interest in finding out about your violin?"

"Yes, he was. And your darling Boris was magnificent, helping out in all sorts of ways in Barcelona. I rather miss his violin. Must ask him to bring it round next time he visits you. He can play to us."

Holly ripped open a bag of designer leaves and scattered them into a bowl. "He'd like that. He'll be round later in the week. I've asked him for supper."

Allegra gave Holly a sidelong glance. "You're growing very fond of him, aren't you?"

"Maybe more," Holly muttered. "I've never felt quite like this about anyone before. Not sure I trust my feelings, though. It's all been so quick."

"And he feels the same?" Allegra asked gently.

"Yes. He says he does. Oh, Allegra, I think I'll

burst if I don't tell you. I think I'm falling in love with him."

"You didn't have to tell me." Allegra drizzled dressing over their salad.

"Oh, sorry," Holly stuttered. "I, I didn't think. Sorry Allegra. I didn't mean to hurt your feelings; oh, how tactless of me, after all the upset you've gone through with Zack..."

"No, silly!" Allegra laughed. "I meant you didn't have to tell me you're falling in love with him because I already know. It's written all over your face every time you talk about him and I'm totally convinced he's the right person for you. No doubt about it."

"Ah." Holly sighed. "I'm relieved. Thought I'd put my foot in it."

"Not at all. Let's eat. Lasagne should be ready now." Allegra pulled a supermarket lasagne out of the oven and plonked it onto the table, next to the salad. "Apparently my dad has mastered home-made lasagne now."

"Impressive!" Holly gave a thumbs up.

"Yes. He made a massive batch of it – Mum had to freeze some. We might get to sample it next week when we're down there."

"It's incredibly kind of your parents to let me stay," Holly said.

"You're more than welcome," Allegra replied. "They've plenty of room now it's just the two of them at home."

"Nevertheless, it's a lot of work to have house

guests," Holly said, "even if we will be out most of the time, over in Bristol."

"I'm looking forward to the concert in St George's," Allegra said. "Should be great fun. I thought we could go down on Monday afternoon and spend the evening with my parents; we won't have to get up too early to be over in Bristol for the rehearsal on the Tuesday."

"Sounds perfect," Holly said as she crunched into a piece of celery. "A bit like this salad."

"Oh I forget to tell you," Allegra said as she passed Holly the garlic bread. "The police contacted me again – said my violin case has turned up at last. The contents have been stripped out, as they suspected they would've been, but the case is still in good shape."

"Good news," Holly said.

"Yes. It doesn't matter about the spare bow – it wasn't worth much – or the strings. All replaceable, except..."

"Except?" Holly raised an eyebrow. "Except what?"

Allegra fiddled with side of the salad bowl. "I had two special photos tucked deep inside the case, under the lining. I'm sorry to have lost them."

"Did the police say they wasn't there?"

"They said the case was completely empty."

"Were the photos of Zack?"

"Yes they were." Allegra's eyes glittered. I'm not going to cry, she thought. Not over photos.

Holly put her hand on Allegra's shoulder and let

it rest there lightly for a minute or two until Allegra recovered.

"One day, when we went to Brighton, we had some of those photos taken in a seaside booth, you know the sort of place," Allegra explained.

Holly nodded.

"There were four photos in a strip, all nearly identical – the two of us, with a funny grey curtain behind. We each kept two photos; I kept mine in my violin case."

"And where is the case?" Holly asked. "Do you have to collect it?"

"That's the funny thing," Allegra said. "The police said the case had been sent over from Spain directly to someone else, who was looking after it on my behalf. One of my friends, apparently, and he's going to bring it round. Told the police he wanted to give me a lovely surprise."

"Must be what's-his-name," Holly said. "You know, your pupil Cassie, her dad. He's a policeman, isn't he?"

"I thought it must be him at first," Allegra said, "but the police said no, it was a musician friend who'd been out in Spain with me when the violin had been stolen. They said they don't usually bother with a stolen case, because it isn't that valuable."

"I see what they mean." Holly chewed thoughtfully. "The police have enough to do without chasing after violin cases. At least they found the actual instrument."

"Exactly."

"But who is this mystery person?" Holly queried. "All sounding a bit elusive."

"Yes! Scarlet Pimpernel?"

"Jonnie English more likely!"

Allegra forked up a helping of salad. "Mm, love radish. Anyway, I'll know soon enough, because they'll bring it round. Oh, Holly, do you think it could be Zack? He hasn't let me know about his job offer, the one in Washington – I know he said he was seriously thinking of accepting it, but he hasn't been in touch to say he's going. I'm assuming no news is good news and he's decided not to take it."

"I'm sure he wouldn't leave without contacting you," Holly said, "not now you're friends again. It wouldn't be fair, would it?"

"Friends don't emigrate without saying anything," Allegra said decisively, "and he said he wanted us to be friends again – we *are* friends again."

Holly leapt up as the bell went. "Are you expecting a pupil?" she asked.

"No," Allegra said. "Are you?"

Holly shook her head. "Maybe it's the mysterious violin case rescuer?"

Holly raced downstairs to the over-sized front door and shrieked with joy when she saw who the visitor was.

"Boris! Come in! We weren't expecting you, but what a lovely surprise!"

"I've got something for Allegra," he said, holding her missing property aloft.

"Come on up," Holly said. "Allegra will be pleased to see her case again!"

"Hello Boris!" Allegra said as he stepped into the tiny hall of their top floor flat in Elgin Court. "How kind of you to bring my case round. Have you eaten?"

"Yes I have, but I could easily eat some more, if you're offering." Boris plonked himself down at the table. "And I expect you're wondering how I've got your case?"

"The police told me it'd been found and a friend would be bringing it round. You are very kind, Boris, to take a personal interest in returning it."

Boris ran his hand through his hair and frowned. "It wasn't quite like that..." he began.

"I'm thrilled!" Allegra said, almost snatching the case from Boris. "I just need to see..."

She pushed her fingers down inside the lining of the case all the way round and even tugged at a loose part of the velvet cloth to look underneath, but in vain. There were no photos.

"Should there be something in there?" Boris asked. "You're searching the case quite thoroughly."

"Wait!" Holly pointed at the velvet. "Look! There's something stuck underneath. See?"

Allegra squealed with joy. "My photos," she said, lifting them to her lips and kissing them.

"What in the world...?" Boris scratched his head.

They were indeed her photos, looking a little the worse for wear, slightly more dog-eared and faded, but still the treasured reminder of happier days. She stuffed them back into the case, suddenly embarrassed at her display of emotion.

Holly whispered something to Boris and the puzzled expression left his face.

"Ah, none of my business, but I think I get it now. However," he added, a fleeting frown appearing again, "I think you might have got the wrong end of the stick."

Allegra looked at him, her emotions under control again – for the time being at least. She couldn't wait to be alone in her room with her photos, to have another look at them, to worship them...besides, something was bothering her. She couldn't put her finger on it. She needed to have another look at those photos as soon as she could and have a think.

"And what stick might that be, Boris?" she asked as she sat down at the table again.

"The sort of stick," Boris said, as he helped himself to a massive portion of pasta and three slices of garlic bread, "that means I do hope you don't think I'm the one who's been chasing your case and arranging for it to turn up here tonight...no, indeed, the credit has to go to someone else entirely."

Allegra's fork stopped in front of her mouth before she had a chance to taste the lasagne and she swallowed, her mouth feeling suddenly dry and uncomfortable. Her heart fluttered like a caged bird. Could it be? Could Zack be her mystery detective and saviour of the case?

Boris coughed. "I don't know if you were aware of this, Allegra, but when we were out in Barcelona, Zack was the one who collaborated with the local police and kept on at them every day, berating them for not finding your violin. He was like a man possessed, completely determined you should have your instrument back."

Allegra's hand flew to her mouth. "I had no idea."

"He went round to the local market every day, convinced your case might turn up there on a bric-a-brac stall. He thought the violin would be long gone, out of the area, but if the case turned up, maybe it would have some clues, fingerprints or what not. He made friends with all the stall holders, giving them his mobile number, so that they could contact him if they saw or heard anything."

"Good gracious!" Holly sat back on her chair, the noise of the legs on the laminate floor piercing the silence as Boris paused in his account to scoff down some more food. "What happened next, Boris? How was it found?"

"Zack's hunch was correct," Boris continued. "A young lad who regularly scavenges the streets for junk and offers it to stall holders to sell on, found the violin case. General feeling is that the thief discarded it pretty quickly, to throw the police off the scent, as a case tends to have personal stuff in. Yours even has your initials engraved on the leather handle – bit of a giveaway. Anyway, the case was found by this lad a couple of days ago, long after the violin had been recovered from the auction; it was down by the river, sheltered by some trees. The contents had been stripped out – except for your photos, obviously, which I have to say were extremely well hidden – and the boy took the case to the stall holder, thinking it might have some second-hand value. It had been out in all weathers – there was no chance of any finger prints or other clues and besides no one needed any more evidence because the violin had already been found and the thief had pleaded guilty. You might even call it an open and shut case?"

"Boris!" Holly shrieked. "That's terrible."

"Thank you," Boris said. "I do my best to please."

"I hope the boy trying to sell the case didn't get into any trouble," Allegra said.

"Yes," Holly agreed. "That wouldn't have been fair at all. He wasn't the thief; he was only trying to raise a bit of money."

"Probably didn't have much and was trying to help his family," Allegra added. "Not everyone's as lucky as we are here, in London."

"Well, actually," Boris said, "here in London there are lots of people...but we're getting off the point. It seems Zack had thought of everything. He'd asked the stall holders to report the case to the police if it was found, and he also left some money for the stall holders to buy the case if it was offered to them and enough money to send it back to England, to his address in Clapham. No doubt he wanted to surprise you one day by bringing it round."

"Thorough," Holly said.

"He was always good at planning," Allegra said dreamily. "You have to be, to conduct an orchestra..."

"And so," Boris chipped in, "the case was sent to Zack. He's the one you should be thanking because, without him, you wouldn't have got your case back – or the violin, come to that."

"But Boris," Holly said, "you played a massive part in getting the violin back. You were the one who recommended putting out information on those websites, to alert the musical community to the fact Allegra's violin had been stolen and might possibly be offered for sale."

"I'd love to take the credit," Boris said, "but again, all down to Zack. I passed on the information to you – he asked me to, and said I should leave his name out of it. Didn't want to take any of the glory but I don't see why I shouldn't tell you now, under the circumstances. I was only partly 'instrumental' in getting your property back – get it? *Instrumental?*"

Holly guffawed to hear further evidence of Boris's wit.

"I owe him so much," Allegra said, her face scarlet. "Why wouldn't he want me to know he was helping?"

"Perhaps," Holly suggested, "he thought if he

offered you the advice, you might have not accepted it, after, after..."

Allegra put her head down.

"Tell you what," Holly said. "Let's have some pudding. Cheesecake or apple crumble?"

"Would it be rude to have both?" Boris licked his lips and Holly swatted him on the shoulder.

"You pig!" she said, snorting with mirth. "Of course it would be rude, but when has that ever stopped you?"

Holly brought the puddings over to the table and Allegra cut into the cheesecake first.

"Here you are, Boris," Holly said, passing him a laden plate. "But there's one thing left I don't understand. Why did you bring the case round? Not that it isn't lovely to see you, of course."

"Yes," Allegra echoed. "Why?"

Boris waved his hand around, to indicate he'd love to talk but currently had his mouth full and as a polite well-brought up member of society, he had no choice but to wait a little longer.

"Ah, an easy question," he managed to say in a minute or so. "Zack asked me to bring the violin case round to you on his behalf. I'm his postman, if you like."

"But why?" Allegra frowned. Was it because he couldn't face her? Or could he not be bothered? He said they were friends – surely he could have popped in with the case? She would have liked to have thanked him for all his efforts. Why did he have to be secretive? Again?

With a growing sense of horror, Allegra realised she probably already knew the answer to her question, knew why Zack hadn't come round, was in fact unable to come round.

Boris halted the progress of a ginormous spoonful of cheesecake on its way to his mouth and confirmed her worst fear.

"Zack couldn't come round because he's on his way to America."

Chapter 19

A Dangerous Discovery

"There's so much to do!"

"Why don't you write one of your famous lists?" Pete suggested. "I know it's a busy day, with Allegra and Holly arriving this evening, but we can get through the chores together. Writing a list seemed to help the other day."

"Ok." Cathy sat down and started scribbling:

Clean whole house.

Food shopping for next few days and cook casserole for this evening.

Pop into garden centre.

Shift at charity shop.

Hoover Maeve's house – still troubled with sciatica.

Go to library to pick up next lot of books for Mrs Oatcake – take round to her house.

Church flowers.

"The whole house doesn't need cleaning – kitchen, bathroom and a quick tidy will suffice," Pete said. "Leave it to me. Don't look so doubtful! And you know Allegra and Holly won't notice. We've seen their flat."

"Nevertheless," Cathy said, "the food shopping

needs doing; you can't convince me *that's* not necessary…"

"I'll do the shopping," Pete said. "And I'll cook the casserole for this evening. What? Not another doubtful look? It's hotpot under another name, isn't it, and you said my hotpot was fine. And if I run out of time, there's still plenty of lasagne in the freezer."

"So there is. And your hotpot was delicious. Ditto the lasagne."

Cathy smiled. Maybe her list wasn't as overwhelming as she'd first thought. Pete was getting on brilliantly with his cooking now and she'd noticed he did much better if she stayed out of his way and let him make decisions. At last, he was settling down into his retirement. About time.

"*Pop into the garden centre* – we can do that chore straight away," Pete said.

"Never got round to picking up a few plants at the weekend, did we?" Cathy said. "I don't want to cross it off the list as it was on the last one, if you see what I mean."

"I do." Pete grinned. "But, there is such a thing as being a slave to the list. It's meant to be an aid, not a dictator."

"Don't exaggerate Pete."

"If I've told you once, I've told you a million times, I never exaggerate…ah, sorry, Cathy. Garden centre's a good idea. Do you know why?"

"I do," Cathy said. "Because they do lovely early morning coffee."

"Spot on! And pastries, don't forget the pastries. What's more, they sell those cakes that can be passed off as home-made."

"Ah yes. Super idea."

"Do you remember when you used to have to make cakes for Allegra when she was at school?"

"Do I! I couldn't keep up with the constant demand from the Parents' Association to send in home baking. They never seemed to consider that people had jobs and didn't want to spend every evening baking for various charity sales, even of it was to raise some cash for the school. And even though all the parents of the children in Allegra's class knew full well I taught at the same school."

"They were a pretty demanding bunch," Pete agreed, "But you made some good friends there too."

"I miss all that," Cathy said, "and I miss my colleagues."

"Anyway, back to the cakes; we managed to come up with a plan to make cakes look homemade, didn't we?" Pete said.

"Buy a shop cake, take it out of the packet, bash it round a bit..."

"...pop some extra icing sugar on," Pete finished. "Fooled them every time. I told my cookery class the whole story last time I went and they all thought it was hilarious. What's more, one by one, they all started admitting they'd done the same sort of thing."

"I often suspected we weren't alone." Cathy

looked at the list again. "All the remaining chores are for other people," she said. "The church, Maeve, Mrs Oatcake..."

Pete grimaced. "Yes they are – what's more, you hoovered for Maeve a few days ago. Why would it need doing again? Has she been having wild parties?"

"She has much higher standards than we do," Cathy explained. "Besides, I didn't manage the whole house, there simply wasn't time. I couldn't do the sitting room properly, because Maeve was in there watching her soap and it would have been painful for her to move."

Pete ran his hands through what was left of his hair until it stood up in angry peaks. "Bet she was scoffing chocolates too," he exploded.

"How did you know?"

"Bitter experience."

"Oh, Pete, it doesn't matter. Please calm down. You know I like to be useful."

After a few deep breaths, Pete said gently "Cathy, maybe you're doing a little too much for other people? I didn't like to say so, but you've been looking a bit tired and run down this autumn – though of course as lovely as ever."

Cathy fiddled with an earring. "I've been worried about Allegra," she admitted. "But yes, I agree. I'm doing too much and feel a bit dragged down by it."

"I know you've been keen for me to start enjoying my retirement," Pete said, "and I think I am now, eventually, in fact I'm having the time of my life at cookery class. Bake-off is my new favourite programme and I've made ever such a lot of new friends – thought I'd have some of them round soon, maybe next week, for Sunday lunch. Don't worry; you won't have to lift a finger."

"That sounds lovely, and I am enjoying my retirement," Cathy said, "but I miss teaching. I'd prefer helping kids to learn their alphabet to doing the church flowers any day, but I don't want to let people down. All my own fault – I took on too many responsibilities as soon as I gave up work. The opposite of what everyone advised."

Pete picked up his mobile. "Leave it with me," he said. "You go and get ready to be whisked away to the garden centre – see what I did there? *Whisked?* A culinary pun; cooking is that close to my heart now..."

Cathy groaned and went up to her bedroom. She couldn't do anything about Pete's terrible sense of humour, but perhaps she could do something to her hair, tame it in some way, before the outing to the garden centre.

Wonder if they have some of those gorgeous autumnal scarlet and mustard blooms, she thought. The ones that supposedly give you colour throughout the transition between summer and winter. Or have I left it too late? Cathy grabbed a bottle of a potion promising to tame her locks and gave her crowning glory a good squirt.

Mm, she thought. Not bad. At least it's got rid of the worst of the 'first Mrs Rochester' look. Let's try some lipstick…better, much better. Blast of perfume and I'm ready to go.

"Why are you looking secretive?" she asked Pete as she joined him in the hall.

"Made a few calls," Pete said. "You're off the hook for the rest of the day."

"You can't go cancelling my commitments without asking." Cathy was horrified. "People depend on me. Pete, this is wrong – I feel guilty."

"I'll tell you all about it once we get going." Pete opened the door and gestured to Cathy to go first. "If I had a cloak, I'd throw it down for you to walk upon," he said. "But as it is, you'll have to dodge the puddles and run to the car."

"This place gets more and more like a village, not a garden centre." Cathy marvelled at the displays of plants, books, kitchen equipment, clothes even, and of course the impressive array of garden furniture.

"Can we look at the sheds?" Pete asked, "I like a good snoop around the sheds and out-buildings."

Cathy beamed. "If you think we've got time."

"We have, my love, because remember I've cleared your duties for the day, well nearly all of them."

"You still haven't said how."

"I rang the church flower rota lady and explained you had visitors coming this evening and were up to your eyes in chores. She said it wouldn't be a problem as they have the Brownies coming in to help today at 4pm; she was adamant that you weren't to worry about it."

"Next I rang the charity shop and they were equally understanding and said you wouldn't be missed – ah, that came out wrong. I didn't mean they wouldn't miss you but they said they'd manage. Again, no problem. Then as I was about to ring Maeve, she rang us."

"Thought I heard the house phone."

"She doesn't need you to hoover any more. She said she's been feeling as if she's been taking you for granted for a long time now."

"Is her sciatica better?"

"Not really but she's invested – her word not mine –*invested* in one of those amazing new-fangled robotic vacuum cleaners. She's having the time of her life watching it whizz round the house. Admittedly it doesn't do the stairs, but it's fantastic on a level surface. Sounds as if she's practically wearing the carpets out; it's having to work very hard. She said we can borrow the appliance whenever we want and suggested this afternoon. What do you think?"

"How kind – dear Maeve – what a smashing idea. And Mrs Oatcake?"

"Ah. Mrs Oatcake." Pete fell silent for a moment. "She's a character, isn't she?"

"One way to describe her."

"I rang her," Pete explained, "but she categorically refused to countenance the idea that you might not be coming round to see her. She said you needn't bring any more books as she's still reading the last lot, but she wants to discuss them with you and would be very upset not to see you today. She asked me to mention she's got some shortbread in."

"Shortbread!" Cathy said. "I'm sure I can spare the time to visit for tea. Thank you Pete, for helping me out. Don't know what I'd do without you."

The two of them spent a happy ten minutes wandering in and out of the outdoor building display, housed in a sunny corner of the garden centre. There were gazebos, and garden rooms, as well as more traditional sheds. Cathy sat on the chair inside an office pod and looked at the space where a computer would go.

"This reminds me of my little office corner in my classroom. I do miss teaching," she said.

"Your phone's ringing."

"Thanks Pete. Didn't notice. Hello? Headmaster! Yes, this is Cathy. Yes, it has been a long time. You like me to what? When? Of course. Half an hour. See you soon!"

"What's going on?" Pete asked.

"They want me back," Cathy said excitedly, "for a few hours, the rest of the day. A teacher has been injured at Shelley Primary – snapped their Achilles tendon which obviously isn't a cause for celebration..."

"Indeed no," Pete said. "Ouch!"

"The new Head's asked me if I would possibly be free to go in and lend a hand; it's the Reception

Class and they can't cover with the staff already there – they've more than enough work to do. He rang me first before he rang the agency for a supply teacher, on the off-chance I could go in."

"Let's be off," Pete said. "What are we waiting for? I'll have you home in a jiffy to collect anything you need, and then run you down to the school. How does that sound?"

In no time at all, Cathy was sitting with the reception class; she gazed at the bright eager faces in front of her, all turned in her direction like a host of sunflowers seeking out the light.

"Now children, what have you brought to show everyone? We're going to have a lovely display on the Nature Table. Don't be shy: who wants to start?"

She smiled at her class while they all put their hands up, even those who had forgotten to bring anything to show. Several children looked as if they might burst with the effort of not calling out.

"Well, that is lovely! I am so pleased with you all. Let's take it in turns to bring our objects up and put them on the table. Here's the first one. A dark red leaf. What a sensational colour! Did anyone else bring leaves? Let's have a look at them. Good. Conkers next: I can see we have a beautiful selection waiting to be shown."

Great quantities of shiny conkers of various sizes were released onto the table and a few immediately skittered off the hard surface and bounced across the floor, much to everyone's amusement.

One little boy held out his hand to Cathy, slowly releasing his fingers one by one, like a petal unfurling, to reveal his surprise.

"Goodness me! I know magpies are supposed to like bright shiny objects – did you find this in a nest?" Cathy asked.

"Course not. It was in me mum's joolery box. I looked in and found this yellow ring with shiny bits stuck in it. D'you like it? Fort it was nicer than a conker or a leaf."

"Yes, I like it very much, but I might put it in this envelope from my desk, that's it; I'll stick the flap down and pop the envelope back in the drawer, then telephone your mum at lunchtime to let her know her ring is safe at school and she can pick it up from me later when she collects you."

Cathy smothered a smile. She was having so much fun.

"Let's move over to the rug by the board," she said. "If you can sit cross-legged, we'll have a little chat about all the interesting objects you've brought in. Is everyone comfortable?"

"Don't like sittin' cross-legged, Miss. Hurts me legs."

"Put your legs to one side then – super! Now, first I'm going to choose an item from the table and whoever brought it in can tell us all about it. What have we here? A photo of a field with a beautiful row of trees at the end and some digging, yes, quite a lot of digging. Who brought this in? Well done. It's a fascinating photo and shows lots of tree roots and a big pipe too. There's a fence round it – looks like a building site. Whereabouts is it? Oh, I know. On the edge of the city. That big area they're developing. I didn't recognise it at first, with the diggers and the trees uprooted. And this is what it looked like yesterday? A fascinating photo and a worthy addition to the nature table. In all my years of teaching, I have to say I don't ever remember anyone bringing in such an interesting photo before. Your brother took it for you? On his phone? And printed it off for you to bring into school. How kind of him."

"Miss, did they have photos when you started teaching?"

"Yes, they certainly did," Cathy said, "but it was much trickier to get the pictures printed out…Yes, there were colour photos, not only black and white. Things were different in 'the olden days', but perhaps not quite as different as you might imagine!"

In her lunch break, when the children were playing outside, Cathy took the chance to photograph the nature table. She thought she would show the photos to Mrs Oatcake when she nipped in for tea on her way home.

"Here it is," Cathy said. "The nature table, in all its glory."

"We used to have a nature table." Mrs Oatcake nodded. "But we didn't bring in photos for it."

"Yes, it was a new one for me," Cathy admitted.

"Wait a minute," Mrs Oatcake said. "What's that weird thing, sticking out of the mud? Show me the photo again. A little bit nearer please; can you enlarge it? More than that? The metal object looks familiar."

"Looks like an old pipe to me," Cathy said, "like something from a farm machine."

"I've seen one of those before, when I was a child. That's not a pipe. It's an unexploded bomb, left over from the War. You need to report it, Cathy. Report it now. It could be deadly dangerous."

Chapter 20

Allegra Counts Her Blessings

"Why are the roads closed? There can't be flooding, can there?" Allegra stopped the car.

"There hasn't been enough rain for flooding," Holly said. "Funny – the sat nav is telling us to go straight on but the road is closed."

Allegra and Holly were on the outskirts of Bath now, driving in from the picturesque road passing Stonehenge, on their way to stay with Cathy and Pete.

"There's a bomb," a stationery motorist ahead shouted. "We have to wait until it's defused."

Holly wound down her window. "Sorry," she said. "I couldn't quite hear you. I thought you said there was a bomb."

"I did. Turn on your radio. We've made the national news. Have to wait here until it's sorted, I guess."

Holly waved her thanks, closed the car window and switched on the radio with trembling fingers.

"An unexploded bomb has been found on a building site just outside Bath, in the West of England...precautionary measures have been put in place …there are road closures and home owners in the immediate vicinity have been asked to leave their homes and go to nearby community centres…"

"A bomb?" Holly said. "There can't be a bomb, not down here, in the West Country."

Allegra switched the car engine off. "Good thing I've got some biscuits," she said.

"Boris has texted," Holly said. "He wants to come down – to see if I'm all right. What a sweetie. I'll tell him there's no need."

"Will they be running trains down to Bath?" Allegra asked.

"The station's nowhere near the evacuation area," Holly answered, studying her phone closely. "I'll read you what it says here, on the BBC news site…please don't worry, Allegra. Your parents will be fine. Everyone will be fine. It's a precaution…"

Allegra's phone beeped with a text from Pete.

No problem here, love. We're both safe. You might have some trouble getting into Bath, but take your time. Your mother discovered the bomb! Long story. Call you when I can.

"Think we need to sing something," Holly remarked. "Remember we used to have a bit of a singsong to cheer ourselves up in the dormitory when we felt a bit homesick at orchestra camp?"

"Good idea. What about 'Keep the home fires burning'?"

Holly giggled. "Little bit inappropriate, with an unexploded World War Two bomb. I was thinking more along the lines of 'Bring me Sunshine'?

"Bring me Sunshine," the two friends started to sing,

"In your smile...

In this world where we live

There should be more happiness..."

"I need to tell you something," Allegra said.

"I knew it!" Holly spun round in her seat to face Allegra. "You've been unnaturally quiet since Saturday evening, when Boris came round to dinner. It's something about the violin case, isn't it? Something's upset you."

"Yes, and no. Not the case. It's the photos."

"The ones hidden under the lining? But I thought you were ecstatic to have got them back again," Holly said.

"I was. I am. But when I found them, they didn't look right." Allegra rubbed her eyes.

"What do you mean, didn't look right?" Holly asked.

"They were the wrong way round."

"The wrong way round?"

"Ae you going to repeat everything I say?" Allegra asked.

"No!"

"I'll start at the beginning of the story – that will be easiest."

"It sure would! Because what you're saying isn't making a whole heap of sense at the moment." Holly sat back in her seat and let out a long breath.

"We've got plenty of time." Allegra said. "By the

look of the traffic building up I've no doubt we'll be stuck here for ages."

"Spit it out," Holly demanded, "but no crying. I can't bear to see you unhappy. Let's have a deal. If you feel like crying, you have to eat another biscuit. OK?"

"OK. I'm going back to the day Zack and I visited Brighton. Oh no. I already feel like having a biscuit." Allegra reached for the custard creams.

"Munch away. And get on with the story – I'm dying of curiosity here. I'll have a biscuit too," Holly said. "No, of course I don't feel like crying. I feel like a biscuit."

"You don't look like one."

"Allegra! Concentrate on your story. Please."

"We had a fantastic time in Brighton," Allegra said. "Spent the whole day larking about on the beach, chasing seagulls, eating ice creams, making plans for the future...Before we went home we spotted one of those seaside photo booths, the ones where you put coins in a slot and they take four photos in rapid succession while you sit there. We thought it'd be fun to have a record of our perfect day."

Holly handed Allegra another biscuit.

"Thanks," she muttered. "We squashed together on the little stool – it was a tight squeeze – and posed, remaining as still as we could. Then we waited outside for the photos to drop out of the machine. You know you're supposed to wait a few minutes for the photos to dry before you handle them? I couldn't wait; I took them out when they were still a bit tacky and put my thumb right in the middle of the set of four, so there was a slight smudge on the two middle photos in the strip. Zack carefully tore the set of photos – he had the top two photos and I had the other two."

"And you kept your photos in your violin case and now you've got them back," Holly said.

"No, I haven't."

"What do you mean?" Holly asked. "I saw them. You've got your photos back. Wait – do you mean…"

"Yes! My photos were the bottom two photos and had the torn strip at the top, with the top photo smudged from my thumb. The photos in the case had the torn strip at the *bottom*, with a smudge on the lower picture. And the pictures are very slightly different, the sort of differences you'd only notice if you'd been studying them for years."

"And you think Zack kept his photos too and swopped them over…do you want a biscuit?"

"No!" Allegra's eyes were shining with excitement. "Don't you see what this means? If he kept his photos all this time, maybe it was because they still meant something to him. As my set of photos meant something, everything, to me."

"The big question is," Holly said, "did he swop them over by mistake?"

"Possibly." Allegra sat motionless in her seat.

"Or was it on purpose?" Holly said. "To send you some sort of message?"

The motorist behind Allegra's car gave a sudden beep and a friendly wave, trying to attract her attention to the fact that the traffic was moving again.

"And we're off," Allegra said. "Talk about this later?"

In twenty minutes, the two friends reached Cathy and Pete's house. As they pulled up outside, Pete rushed out to greet them.

"Thank goodness," he exclaimed. "It's all over at last; they've defused the bomb. Your mother's quite shaken. I had to go and collect her from Mrs Oatcake's house."

"Who's Mrs Oatcake?" Allegra asked as she hugged her dad.

"I forgot you didn't know her," Pete said. "Hello Holly! Lovely to see you. Come in, both of you. Mrs Oatcake's here too. She refused to be left out, and Maeve's here as well. It's quite a party. Like the war spirit, Mrs Oatcake says. She's been telling us stories from her childhood about bombs and heroism. Apparently her father was a doctor in Birmingham during the war – he was given the George Medal by the King for his heroic deeds. Even Maeve is impressed."

Very soon, Holly and Allegra were sitting cosily with Pete, Cathy, Maeve and Mrs Oatcake.

"Tell us more about it, Mum," Allegra begged. "The whole story, from beginning to end..."

"...and the end," Cathy said, "is that the headmaster rang a little while ago. He's offered me a job, very part-time, two afternoons a week, but just what I want."

"I thought you'd retired," Holly said.

"Yes, but it's complicated," Cathy began.

"Cathy wasn't enjoying retirement as much as she thought she would," Pete said. "She missed teaching too much."

"This is the perfect solution," Maeve chipped in. "You'll have time for the charity shop..."

"Your volunteer reading..." Mrs Oatcake added.

"While having time with the kids at school," Cathy said.

"...and still having time to yourself," Pete added in a stern sort of voice, looking round the group, his gaze lingering on Maeve and Mrs Oatcake.

"Indeed," Maeve agreed.

"Yes," Mrs Oatcake said. "Message received. Loud and clear. Roger and out."

"I might give up church flowers," Cathy said, "and Pete's taking over the shopping and cooking."

Allegra looked at her parents' contented faces and felt delighted. She'd had faith all along they'd sort things out. They were a team. She suppressed all thoughts of Zack. No point in thinking about him and whether she and he would have ever made a good team. All in the past. Despite what she'd said to Holly in the car, about maybe Zack wanting to send her a message by swopping over the photos, she knew it was unlikely. He'd obviously searched the case when he got it back for her, found the photos and replaced them by mistake with the other set he had. He must have kept his photos by chance – he wasn't great at sorting out his hoards of stuff and tended to hang on to the most unlikely items long after they should have been discarded.

Except me. He didn't hang on to me.

"May I have a word, Allegra?" Maeve asked. "In the kitchen?"

"Of course," Allegra said, surprised.

"This is difficult," Maeve said, "but I feel I owe you an apology. I've owed it to you for a long time and now, to see you sitting there, looking peaky and tired..."

Allegra said nothing. She knew Maeve could be tactless and she might as well let her get on with whatever apology she was about to make.

"The thing is," Maeve began, "I think I expressed my opinion too strongly."

"What about?"

"Zack. When you were engaged, I remember I expressed opinions on subjects that were none of my business. I don't know much about men, never having been lucky enough to have met the right person and settle down to a loving family life like your dear parents, and so even more I shouldn't have expressed my opinion to you about Zack. I remember saying something rash about him needing to sort out his priorities and I had no right to do so. I'm mortified and desperately sorry if it had an impact on your relationship. It was unforgivable."

"Please don't worry," Allegra said. "I managed to mess up my relationship with Zack all by myself. No one else's fault."

"Nevertheless dear, I feel better for having got that off my chest, after all this time. Now, shall we rejoin the others? Oh, here's Mrs Oatcake."

"Might I have a word, Allegra dear," Mrs Oatcake said. "In private," she added, staring at Maeve.

"I'll make myself scarce," Maeve said with a chuckle. "You're very popular today."

"I wanted to tell you, Allegra," Mrs Oatcake said, "that when you're young, you should be having lots of fun. Your father's been telling me he thinks you are married to your violin, but what I have to say is this: I think it would be much more fun to be married to a nice young man, maybe that Zack your mother's told me about?"

Goodness, Allegra thought. Was there nothing else for people in Bath to think about other than the failed romance between her and Zack? Taking Mrs Oatcake's advice in the kindly spirit it was meant, she murmured, "I'm sure you're right."

"Allegra!" Maeve said. "Come back into the sitting room. Have I shown you my robotic vacuum cleaner? No? Here, you have a try. The controls are very easy. See? Diverting, isn't it?"

Allegra pressed a button and watched the fearsome plastic beast tearing around her parents' carpet, munching up crumbs and dust.

"Boris!" Holly's cry could be heard over the crackling sound of the robot vacuum.

Allegra rushed through to the hall and found Holly embracing Boris.

"I had to come down," he said. "It's a quick journey – an hour and a half on the train from Paddington – and I had to make sure you were all right. You are all right, aren't you, my darling Holly? Because I simply couldn't bear it – if you weren't all right."

"More than all right," Holly said as she allowed Boris to envelop her in a comforting hug.

"Ah," Mrs Oatcake said, as she tottered into the hall. "See what I mean. Allegra? Lots of fun."

"They're talking about it on the radio now," Pete called from the sitting room, "about how they managed to defuse the bomb and avert the danger. It could have been terrible...come in here and listen everyone!"

"I'm so glad it's all over," Cathy commented as she budged up on the sofa to accommodate the crowd.

"We owe everything to the bomb squad," Maeve declared.

"What about the boy who found the bomb?" Cathy reminded her.

"Yes," Holly said. "If he hadn't thought that field looked interesting and asked his brother to take a photo..."

"If you hadn't showed me the picture of the nature table..." Mrs Oatcake said to Cathy.

"If you hadn't remembered what a bomb looked like, from the War..." Pete said to Mrs Oatcake.

"Team effort!" Boris yelled and everyone

cheered.

Allegra relaxed, stretching her legs out in front of her. She was content and happy to be among friends and family. There was so much to be grateful for. Life wasn't like a story. Love didn't always work out. Maybe there'd be someone for her, one day, but she would have to wait and see.

For now, it was enough to be grateful for what she had and for the fact they were all safe, after a very frightening time.

Chapter 21

A Second Chance
Ten weeks later – December

It was nearly Christmas and the weather forecast that morning had mentioned the possibility of snow. Allegra shuffled along, squeezing through the crowds at Waterloo Station, anxious to stride out and get some air. She walked quickly over the Golden Jubilee Bridge, taking in the bright skyscrapers with their strange new shapes and the shiny sparkling river below. She was looking forward to this evening.

A tremendous opportunity had fallen into her lap, the chance to play a solo at St Martin-in-the-Fields, 'The Lark Ascending', one of her all-time favourite pieces. She walked past Charing Cross and made her way through the side of Trafalgar Square to St Martin's.

Her parents and other friends coming to the concert would arrive later. She always liked to make her own way to a solo performance, finding it the best solution to coping with her nerves.

She went downstairs to her dressing room and took out her violin, tuning it carefully and running through a few phrases, sending her mind deep into the piece she was about to perform, imagining the lark taking its flight across the beautiful countryside.

Changing into her concert dress, she felt her fluttering nerves turn to excitement and anticipation of the concert. She could hear other musicians arriving and several members of the orchestra popped their heads round the door to wish her luck

"Not that you'll need it – the rehearsal this morning was fabulous."

And now I'm climbing the steep steps, making my way up to the side of the stage area. I'm walking in, the orchestra are on their feet...

"Ladies and Gentlemen, I'd like to say a few words before I play. First of all, I want to tell you what a very great pleasure it is to be here this evening and to have the chance to play 'The Lark Ascending' to you. I've played it many times, in many different venues – I've even played it at a friend's wedding.

"I hope we have a quiet evening tonight because the last time I played 'The Lark Ascending' in central London, there was a Chinook helicopter flying overhead, adding its own special sounds to the performance. A sort of 'Urban Lark'!

But seriously, this has to be one of the most beautiful pieces ever written – a nostalgic reminder of the past, of summer, warmth, tenderness and the countryside. I'm honoured to perform it for you tonight. Ladies and gentlemen, 'The Lark Ascending'."

I pull my bow across the strings to check the tuning for the last time; satisfied, I turn to the conductor and nod. I can see my parents in the front row, Mum with her nails digging into the palm of one hand, thinking I don't know she does that every time she's ever watched me play a solo since I was six years old. And Dad, dear Dad, with an expression on his face that is both incredibly soppy and incredibly proud all at the same time.

Boris and Holly are here, holding hands – and I can see Cassie and her parents. Maeve and Mrs Oatcake too – can't believe they've both made the journey up to London to hear me. I'm so grateful.

And Zack's coming in at the back of the church – I can see him, in a dark overcoat, brushing a few flakes of snow from his shoulders, except I know he isn't here. I imagine him. I see him everywhere, in the street, in cafés and art galleries but every time the figure turns round, it's someone else, his shadow, my mind playing tricks.

The orchestra whispers the opening soft plump chords, like a nest for my lark. First trembling little flurries, then bolder, until up flies the bird, soaring, blossoming, up, up into the beautiful wedding cake roof above, the stunning white plaster and gold leaf. The audience hold their breath and we're off on a wonderful lyrical flight to the heavens. I close my eyes. The melodies unfold and float through the air, filling the hall with the sweetest fragrance imaginable.

I think back to the letter I received from Zack last month. He put several enormous leaves in the envelope, in colours brighter than I've ever seen in nature before in this country; so vivid – scarlet, vermillion, bright orange, fiery red – a real taste of Virginia.

He said he wants me to forgive him for everything, for all the mistakes, but how can I, when the mistakes are all mine?

Finally, he's at peace with his adoption. He has two families now, and soon, he said, when the time is right, he'll come back to England, to live here again.

His birth mother knows all about me and she wants to meet me. As for the photos, he said it was only when he found them inside the case, after it was sent over from Spain, that he fully realised I must still have feelings for him. He understood that if I'd kept them close at hand all those years we were apart, safe in my violin case, it must mean he still had a special place in my heart.

The amazing thing is, he kept his photos too. Treasured them. He said he always carried them round in his wallet, which is why they are as dog-eared as mine. He swopped my photos with his photos, hoping I'd notice.

Now he carries my photos and I have his.

When he comes back, if it works out, it will be a second chance for us both. A chance to get things right. A chance for true love. I've no idea how long it will take for him to be ready to love me again. But I'll be waiting. However long it takes. Love will find its way. Dear

Zack. I love him so much.

The music's drawing to an end now; the beautiful fluttering is quietening and settling.

At the end of Allegra's solo, the audience sat still, poised for the right time, waiting until they could wait no longer, then jumped to their feet.

"Bravo!"

"Encore!"

"Superb!"

Allegra was presented with flowers and called back many times by the ecstatic crowd. Finally, she was released to go back down to the dressing room, the cheering ringing in her ears. She wanted to put her violin away and rush to join her parents and friends. But what was this? The door of the dressing room was ajar and her violin case open. She looked in the case and saw the two sets of photos, hers and Zack's, lying next to each other. Zack's grandmother's ruby ring was sitting beside the photographs.

"Vanessa decided she didn't want it." Zack was standing in the doorway, his wide shoulders blocking the light from the corridor, looking impossible handsome.

"She wants to marry my brother Joe all right, and they're well suited, should be very happy, but both she and Joe wanted me to have the ring back. They'd never felt comfortable about having it and thought it should be returned so that I could give it to the person I want to be my wife, the person I love more than anyone in the world, the person I adore and want to spend the rest of my life with."

Allegra's face lit up and in an instant Zack was by her side.

"You performed beautifully," he said in a hoarse voice, then kissed her so tenderly, she thought she'd gone to heaven.

The two of them clung to each other.

"I thought I saw you at the back, but wasn't sure if I'd imagined it. Zack, I've missed you so much. We've been..."

"...total idiots? Haven't we just. I can't believe I left you to rush off to America without a proper explanation."

"But you sent me the letter."

"And you replied." Zack grinned.

"And our photos are back together, where they belong."

"Never to be parted. We should frame them. Hang them over the mantelpiece."

Allegra nestled happily in Zack's arms while he stroked her hair and kissed the top of her head.

"Are you back for good?" she asked.

"Yes. I've given my notice in, at the University. It was great staying with my mother and her family, but now I want to pick up where I left off, if that's all right with you?"

"Do you mean...?"

Zack smiled. "Let's not bother with all the explanations. We both know what we mean. I love you, darling Allegra. Just answer me one quick question."

"Gladly."

"Allegra, will you marry me?"

How I've longed to hear these words again, to have this second chance.

"Yes! Yes, Zack. Of course I'll marry you."

He slips the ring onto the third finger of my left hand – where, this time, it will stay.

About The Author

Jenny Worstall

Jenny is a writer and musician living in South London with her family. You will find her playing the piano, singing in a choir or gossiping with her friends (essential research for her writing).

She is a member of the Romantic Novelists' Association and the Society of Women Writers and Journalists.

Her writing reflects her love of music and a tendency not to take life too seriously.

If you have enjoyed this book or any other book by Jenny Worstall, why not leave a review on Amazon? It's easy to do and doesn't have to be long — who knows, you might help another reader discover Jenny's books!

Printed in Great Britain
by Amazon